"There is no one ... he assured her.

She was looking at him suspiciously. "I won't be a party to some other woman getting hurt over infidelity."

"Scout's honor," he said with a straight face.

She seemed to be satisfied with his answer. "Okay, then. What happens here stays here."

"Done," he promised.

"You can't tell anyone about our hooking up tonight. No one at all."

"Understood," he wholeheartedly agreed. "That goes for you, too. Not even your girlfriends."

"Not even your boys," she countered.

"Not even your priest," he said.

"Not even God," she said with a smile.

"I think He already knows," said Colton as he backed her against the wall and planted a sensual, bone-melting kiss on her sweet mouth.

Their bodies pressed closer and warmth ensued shortly afterward. By some silent consensus they agreed that this seduction would be slow and deliberate. When they came up for air from that first kiss, their eyes met and they smiled. It was confirmed: they were a good fit.

Books by Janice Sims

Harlequin Kimani Romance

Temptation's Song
Temptation's Kiss
Dance of Temptation
A Little Holiday Temptation
Escape with Me
This Winter Night

JANICE SIMS

is the author of twenty-two novels and has had stories included in nine anthologies. She is the recipient of an Emma Award for her novel *Desert Heat* and two Romance in Color awards: an Award of Excellence for her novel *For Keeps* and a Best Novella award for her short story in the anthology *A Very Special Love.* She has been nominated for a Career Achievement Award by *RT Book Reviews* and her novel *Temptation's Song* was nominated for Best Kimani Romance Series in 2010 by *RT Book Reviews.* A longtime member of Romance Writers of America, she lives in Central Florida with her family.

This Winter Night

Janice Sims

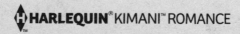

HARLEQUIN® KIMANI™ ROMANCE

Recycling programs
for this product may
not exist in your area.

ISBN-13: 978-0-373-86324-2

THIS WINTER NIGHT

Copyright © 2013 by Janice Sims

For questions and comments about the quality of this book, please contact us at CustomerService@Harlequin.com.

Printed in U.S.A.

Dear Reader,

This Winter Night is the first book in a new series. I wondered what effect a domineering mother would have on her five daughters. She believes her influence helped produce an architect, a zoologist, an accountant, a psychotherapist and a helicopter pilot. But was it at the detriment of personal relationships? It will take a special kind of man to reach the hearts of the Gaines sisters. I hope you enjoy Lauren's story and will look for Desiree's, Petra's, Amina's and Meghan's stories in the near future.

If, after reading *This Winter Night*, you'd like to send me a message, you can email me at Jani569432@aol.com or visit my website, www.janicesims.com. You can also find me on Facebook.

If you're not online, you can write me at P.O. Box 811, Mascotte, FL 34753-0811.

Best,

Janice Sims

Thanks to my usual support team: Shannon Criss for her editorial expertise; Maria Ribas and the rest of the staff at Harlequin who make writing a pleasure; Sha-Shana Crichton for ensuring I have interesting work to keep me busy; and my family for their love and encouragement.

Chapter 1

Colton Riley knew a fool when he saw one. At that moment, he happened to be looking at the fool in his rearview mirror. What had he been thinking? He had driven to the Great Smoky Mountains in the midst of winter without first checking a weather report.

It was snowing so aggressively visibility was practically nonexistent. If not for GPS, he would have gotten lost, even though he'd traveled this route many times before.

He put the SUV in Park as he pulled in front of the cabin with its headlights trained on the porch. He hadn't been there in a long time but he knew there was a spare set of keys somewhere in the car. After a quick search he found them in the glove compartment, zipped his jacket all the way up to his chin and got out of the vehicle.

The fierce north wind whipped snow in his face. The temperature, which had dipped drastically since he'd left Raleigh, North Carolina, for Bryson City, a little town near the Tennessee border, chilled him to the bone. His father's recent death had been such a shock to the system he wasn't his normal rational self. Otherwise, he would have worn a heavier coat— perhaps rethought this entire trip completely.

He unlocked the cabin's front door and took a couple steps inside where he automatically reached for the light switch. He pressed the flat panel but was rewarded with no illumination whatsoever. Then he remembered the alarm and rushed over to the unit but found even the green ready light was out. Power failure. He then made his way to the kitchen where he found a flashlight in the drawer next to the stove. Switching it on, he headed to check the breaker box in the laundry room at the back of the cabin. It was as he suspected—there was no electricity in the cabin. Probably downed power lines due to the blizzard, he thought grimly. He now regretted not having backup generators put in the cabin according to his parents' objections. They liked the austerity of the place. Said they came to the mountains to get away from the modern world as much as possible. Besides, they frequented the cabin more often in warmer months than in the dead of winter, so they figured they didn't need a generator.

Next he checked the cubbyhole in the mudroom

where his parents kept logs for the fireplace. Empty. That did it. He would not survive the night in a cabin without electricity in the middle of a snowstorm, not when there wasn't the remotest prospect of a roaring fire.

He made his way back through the cabin and out the front door. He suddenly remembered glancing at the fuel gauge in the SUV before he had gotten out earlier and again realized that the tank was nearly empty. He laughed roughly. His dad would have probably gotten a good laugh out of this experience for years. Be prepared for anything, he'd always said. *Well, Dad,* Colton thought, *I wasn't prepared for you dying. That kind of threw me for a loop.*

He climbed back in the SUV. Luckily, he hadn't been in the cabin long enough for the snow to freeze on the windshield. The wipers cleared away the accumulation, and he spied the cabin across the pond. Lights shone in its windows. The property belonged to Adam Eckhart. His parents had been reluctant to tell him of the purchase three years ago when his biggest business rival had "coincidentally" moved next door to the Riley family cabin. Colton had simply laughed at the time because he rarely went to the mountains. His parents had frequented the cabin more than anyone else in their family.

It made him wonder, though, just what kind of psychological games Adam was playing with him. The man clearly had no sense of business fairness. At least twice Eckhart had used underhanded methods to push

Colton's construction company out of the bidding for lucrative contracts.

One of the city officials whose palms Eckhart had greased had even come to Colton and boldly said things might go his way if his gift were larger than Eckhart's had been. But the Riley family didn't conduct business in that manner. So Eckhart had gotten the contract.

Looking at the Eckhart cabin now, Colton was resigned to the fact that beggars couldn't be choosers. He would have to go knocking on his enemy's door tonight, or freeze.

Lauren Gaines-Eckhart luxuriated in the warm, soapy water of the sunken tub. She had pinned up her long, wavy raven's-wing-colored hair to keep it dry, and put a Ben Harper CD in the sound system in an attempt to banish all thoughts of Adam Eckhart. She peered up at the clock on the wall. They had now been divorced exactly three days, seven hours and thirty-six minutes. She grimaced. Sometimes she was too anal for her own good.

"Ben, Ben," she moaned. "Take me away!" But the sound of Ben Harper's beautiful voice wasn't working tonight. Like bile, hatred for her ex-husband coursed through her taut body. The more she tried to relax, the more images of doing violence to Adam flashed through her mind.

She smiled at the thought and sank deeper in the tub as she laid her head on the pillow. Finally she relaxed. As Ben Harper's sweet tenor soared she closed her eyes. Tomorrow she would think about making her way back to Raleigh for work, family and responsibility, but for tonight, Christmas Eve, she was fine with being cut off from everyone and everything in her life. She'd been in the mountains for two days and had stayed in spite of severe weather warnings that mentioned the likelihood of a blizzard. She felt safe here. As an architect, she'd designed the cabin with backup generators that would provide power for several days, insulated windows and a reinforced roof built to withstand the weight of heavy snowfall. This cabin was safer than some military installations. The daughter of a retired U.S. Army general, she knew a little about the military.

As an added bonus, her nosy sisters wouldn't be able to travel up there to commiserate with her about her divorce. She adored all four of them and knew they meant well but they wouldn't let her wallow and she wanted to wallow, at least for a few days. Then, like everyone expected of her, she would pull herself together and get on with her life.

She felt her muscles loosen and sighed contentedly. A delicious feeling of peace suffused her body. Then, just as quickly, her muscles tightened once again. Was that the doorbell? She glanced at the clock—9:25 p.m.? Who in their right mind would be out and about during a snowstorm?

She sat up in the tub and listened. There it was again, this time followed by someone pounding like crazy on her front door.

Curious, and a little ticked off by the intrusion, she

rose. Tall and curvy, her brown body glistened with water droplets. Carefully, she stepped onto the plush bath rug and grabbed a towel to quickly dry off.

Pulling on her robe and slippers, she hurried into the adjacent bedroom and went straight to the closet. Pushing aside some clothes she revealed a wall safe. She quickly put in the combination, opened it and removed the semiautomatic she kept for self-defense.

Her father had made sure that all his daughters knew how to safely use a handgun. She loaded it and made sure the safety was engaged. She didn't want to accidentally shoot anyone. She would fire the weapon only if it became necessary to defend herself—a woman couldn't be too careful here in the isolated mountains. The nearest police station was miles away. And no one was going to come to her rescue in a blizzard.

Colton pressed his ear to the door as he strained to hear any forthcoming footsteps from within. Could Eckhart have programmed the lights to come on at regular intervals to deter thieves? If so, the cabin could be unoccupied. He tossed that theory aside. The power was out. If the power were out in his family's cabin, the power would be out in Eckhart's, as well. Even with backup generators, someone would have to manually start them up, right? At least he hoped so.

He was about to start pounding on the door again when a feminine voice yelled, "Identify yourself, and quickly!"

"My name is Colton Riley. My family owns the cabin across the pond..."

"I know Frank and Veronica Riley," said the voice impatiently. "Stand back so I can see your face."

Colton took a step backward. He was trembling with cold, his arms wrapped around his jacket in an attempt to hold in what little body heat he had left.

Inside, Lauren squinted as she perused his face. Yes, although they'd never formally met, she recognized Colton Riley's clean-shaven chiseled features from various charitable events they'd both attended, and from family photographs his mother, Veronica, had shown her over the years. She was clearly proud of her son and had talked about him a lot. Also, it was hard not to recognize the man her ex-husband detested. He'd bought this cabin just to irk Colton Riley. Lauren had wondered about her husband's sanity then—to buy a cabin just to rub somebody else's nose in it. The fact that he was so rich that he could move right next door to a sworn enemy and they had no control over it whatsoever. On the other hand, gaining ownership of the cabin in the divorce was a breeze because Adam hadn't gotten the rise out of Colton Riley he'd expected when he'd bought the property. He'd been summarily ignored. So when Lauren had said she wanted the cabin he hadn't put up a fight.

Now his business rival was standing on her doorstep wanting to come inside out of the cold.

"Okay, you're Colton Riley. What do you want?" she yelled.

Sure she recognized him, but who knew, he might moonlight as a serial killer on weekends.

Exasperated and freezing, Colton got riled. "Look, my dad died earlier today and, not thinking clearly, I got in my car and just started driving, going nowhere in particular. Then I looked up and realized I was headed here. So…"

Lauren had the door open and was yanking him inside before he could finish his sentence. Colton was so grateful to feel the rush of warm air on his skin he collapsed onto the floor in a snow-covered heap. Lauren shut the door but not before the blustery conditions blew snow onto the polished wood floor. She gazed down at her uninvited guest. "Frank passed away?"

Colton's eyes met hers. In hers he saw shock and sympathy.

He stood up. He was at least six inches taller than she was and she wasn't a small-statured woman—five-eight, maybe five-nine. "Yeah, of pancreatic cancer. Kept it quiet for years. He didn't want anyone feeling sorry for him."

There were tears in her eyes. She stood there with a towel wrapped around her hair and dressed in a bathrobe with pink bunny slippers on her feet. She should have looked comical, even ridiculous, but instead she looked beautiful to him. Not just beautiful—angelic.

It could have something to do with the fact that she'd just saved his life by letting him in, he thought skeptically. "Please, don't cry," he said softly as he rubbed his arms to speed up his body's recovery from the cold.

Lauren wiped the tears away with her free hand and seeing he was severely underdressed for the weather outside and must be freezing, she sprang into action.

"Come with me," she told him, and began walking toward the back of the cabin.

"Is that a gun?" he asked cautiously after catching sight of the weapon she held at her side.

"A girl has to stay safe," she said offhandedly.

"So, it's true what they say about you Gaines girls," Colton said as he followed her.

Lauren smiled over her shoulder at him. She had been under the impression he knew nothing of her background. But apparently her reputation, or to be more accurate, her father's reputation, had preceded her.

"What do they say about us Gaines girls?"

"That you don't mess with the general's daughters."

She laughed shortly. "Damned straight, you don't."

She led him to the guest room and switched on the light. She gestured to the closet. "I'm sure some of the clothes in there should fit you. There are towels and toiletries in the bathroom. By the time you're finished taking a hot shower I'll have something warm for you to eat and drink."

Although grateful, Colton hesitated to accept her generous offer. He stood peering down into her up-turned face, an expression of surprise on his own. "Are you sure this is okay with your husband?"

He wanted to avoid being caught naked in the shower by an irascible husband who'd stalked in from somewhere else in the house.

"Ex-husband," Lauren informed him tightly.

He looked confused. "I'm sorry. I didn't know."

"Nondisclosure clause in the prenuptial," Lauren said briskly. "I can't speak to the media about our divorce or about anything that happened in our marriage. He thinks it might reflect negatively on him, from a business standpoint. Now, I'll leave you alone."

She left before he could say anything else, closing the door firmly behind her.

Colton looked around the spacious room with its pine floor, vaulted ceiling with exposed beams, and a natural stone fireplace. He'd heard she was an architect. As a builder he could see the thought and skill that had gone into its design.

Right now, though, a nice warm shower was what he needed. He wasted no more time peeling off his clothes and stepping into a steamy bath.

Having taken the time to put on jeans and a long-sleeved cotton shirt, Lauren stood in the kitchen, heating up some of her hearty beef vegetable soup she'd made earlier that day. As she stirred it with a wooden spoon, she wondered how Veronica was doing. Veronica and Frank had to have been married nearly forty years. What did you do when you lost someone you'd been with for that long? Someone you adored? Frank had a reputation for being a hardnosed businessman but with Veronica he'd been nothing but loving. The time Lauren had spent with them up in the mountains, sharing meals and playing chess with Frank who once told her that she and Veronica were the only women who'd ever bested him at the game, would now be dearly cherished memories.

Their son, though, was a mystery. She knew only what others had told her about him. He'd taken over the company when his father had retired. The Rileys had been in the construction business for more than half a century in the Raleigh area. They were known for being trustworthy and for producing quality private homes and commercial buildings. On the other side, Lauren had spent the entire length of her marriage listening to Adam complain about "those damned Rileys" who "have had a monopoly in this city for too long." Adam was the upstart, and in order for the newcomer to triumph over the standard-bearer, deals were made that might be conceived as manipulative, perhaps even downright illegal. In return, Lauren had started to dislike her ex-husband long before she discovered he was having an affair.

Back in the guest room, Colton had showered and brushed his teeth, and then found a pair of jeans that would fit him and a soft denim shirt in the closet. No underwear, which was fine with him. Unless he found a pair of briefs fresh out of the package, he wouldn't be wearing anything that had once been *that* close to Adam Eckhart's body.

He did find a package of thick, white athletic socks, which he opened, selected a pair and pulled onto his feet. Appropriately dressed now, he went in search of his hostess. He let his nose lead him to the kitchen. Whatever she was cooking smelled wonderful. He hadn't realized how hungry he was. He'd left Raleigh

hours ago, his trip a meandering blackout until he recognized some familiar landmarks and realized he was
headed to the family cabin, a place where he'd spent
many an idyllic summer fishing, swimming, hiking
and kayaking and generally making his older sister,
Jade's, life miserable. She'd been such a neat freak that
he'd gotten a kick out of throwing her in the pond, or
putting frogs, snakes and insects in her bed. He'd been
a total jerk to her back then. It was a wonder they had
such a close, loving relationship today. He'd left Jade
in Raleigh with their mother. Which reminded him, by
now they must be worried sick about him. He needed
to call and tell them that he was fine. He felt bad for
making them worry on top of the grief they were feeling due to his father's recent death.

Where was his cell phone? He found his jacket by
the front door where Lauren had hung it on the coat
tree to allow it to dry. He rummaged through the damp
pockets until he found it. No lit-up display indicated
it was in need of a recharge.

A few seconds later, he was walking through the
kitchen doorway. Spotting Lauren ladling soup into a
bowl, he said, "Thanks. I think my body temp's back
to normal again."

She looked up and smiled, "Good. You're not a vegetarian, are you? I've got some beef vegetable soup.
Would you like coffee? Or maybe hot chocolate?"

Colton sat down at the place setting she'd provided
for him at the high-counter kitchen island. "No, I'm
definitely not a vegetarian. That soup sounds good.
And a hot chocolate, please," he said. "Thank you…"

"Call me Lauren."

She smiled again, and his heart skipped a beat. He hoped he wasn't becoming infatuated with Adam Eckhart's ex. It didn't help that the woman was kind and generous to a fault. She was also drop-dead gorgeous with her fresh face, skin so clear and golden-brown with a hint of red as if she was blushing underneath. She'd taken the towel off her head and her blue-black hair fell in waves about her heart-shaped face. She was adorable without makeup. He'd seen her all dressed up at the Black and White Ball last year. She'd been on Eckhart's arm with him beaming like an idiot, and no wonder—she'd been the belle of the ball. She'd been breathtaking then but not as appealing as she looked now, so vulnerable, as if her emotions were barely being contained. He supposed she was hurting from the divorce. Could that be why she was up here alone—contemplating her lost marriage? He would not broach the subject. Even if he'd known her for more than an hour, which he hadn't, he would never bring it up.

"This looks good," he said just before sampling the soup. It was savory with a tomato base, tender chunks of beef, and just the right amount of red pepper for spice. He looked up at her with appreciation. "You made this?"

"Homemade," she confirmed with a smile.

"Delicious," he said.

"I'm glad you like it," Lauren said softly as she busied herself making hot chocolate.

Momentarily, Colton put down his spoon and regarded her. "I'm sorry for intruding on your downtime. But when I got to the cabin I found out there was no electricity, and no wood for a fire, so I had no other choice but to come knocking on your door."

She was smiling as she poured hot milk into two mugs. "You don't have to explain. I know Veronica and Frank never had backup generators put in. I tried to convince them to but they insisted their place was more rustic and somehow more romantic without the generators."

She stirred cocoa, sugar and a touch of vanilla into each mug. "They were the perfect couple."

Colton cleared his throat when he felt a lump forming in it, and tears at the backs of his eyes. He couldn't start bawling in front of a stranger, even if she was a sympathetic stranger.

He took a deep breath. "Yeah, they were pretty devoted to each other."

Lauren placed a mug of hot chocolate in front of him and sat down across from him at the kitchen's island. "You don't have to talk if you don't want to. I understand. I got out of Raleigh shortly after I got word my divorce was final. I wanted time to myself before my family began to smother me, wanting to know if I was all right."

He noticed she spoke with a smile that didn't reach her eyes, which by contrast were sad. Because he didn't like her ex-husband he couldn't imagine a woman not being overcome with joy after being declared free and clear of the buffoon.

He ate his soup in silence as she sipped her hot chocolate.

Although neither of them actually looked at the other, there were a lot of quick secret glances. Lauren had noticed his short, naturally dark brown hair was still damp from the shower and he had strong hands. He ate slowly, savoring each bite, which made her wonder if he did other things in that manner, as well. No rush, just lingering and appreciating, enjoying the moment. His skin was the color of cinnamon, and his eyes were dark gray, like his father's. His photographs didn't do him much justice, and the few times she'd seen him at public functions she had not given him much thought because after all she had been a married woman.

Colton could not help inhaling the clean feminine scent of her. Fresh out of a bath, he figured since she had opened the door in her bathrobe. Even half-frozen, he hadn't missed that. Her silhouette was classically beautiful, the slender neck, that square chin with the dimple in its center, angling up to a full mouth with lips that looked soft and inviting. Damned if a near-death experience didn't make you more observant, and appreciative, of things you might never have noticed before. When she breathed in and out, he imagined her full breasts heaving with desire, for him.

Once or twice while he was finishing his meal they smiled at one another, but uttered not a word. When he was done with the soup, he looked up at her. "That was wonderful. You saved me."

Lauren laughed nervously as her eyes met his. "What was I supposed to do, let you freeze to death?"

His gaze went to her mouth. Her tongue flicked out and moistened her lower lip. She rose and reached for his bowl. "Can I get you some more?"

Suddenly, his heart was thudding in his chest, and his manhood, already going commando in his borrowed jeans, began to stir. He knew he had to get out of her presence before he said or did something that would embarrass them both.

"Um, no, thank you. I think I'll just go to bed. I'm more tired than I thought."

If he wasn't mistaken, she looked relieved at his announcement. Was she feeling the same attraction he was feeling?

"Of course," she said, hurriedly crossing the room to put the bowl in the sink. "You know the way. If you need an extra blanket, they're on the top shelf in the closet."

"Good night, then, and thank you," Colton said hoarsely.

"Good night," she said softly, chancing a shy glance in his direction. "Hopefully, we'll have better weather tomorrow."

Chapter 2

Colton got all the way to the door of the guest room before he realized he hadn't asked Lauren if the phones were working. He could not with good conscience go to bed without attempting to let his family know he was safe.

Lauren was washing dishes at the sink when he returned to the kitchen. She heard him enter and placed a dish on the draining board before turning to face him. "Is there a problem?"

"My cell phone's out of juice and I have no way of recharging it. Do you have a working phone I can use?"

She was drying her hands on a dish towel as she walked toward him. "The landline's down due to the storm, but I have a satellite phone you can use."

"A satellite phone?" Colton mused. "You have to be outside when you use that, right, underneath open sky?"

"Mmm-hmm," Lauren confirmed with a smile. "I take it with me when I hike in the woods or the mountains."

She hung the dish towel on a rack attached to the oven door and walked over to the large window in the kitchen and drew aside the curtains. The wind had died down and it wasn't snowing any longer. Colton joined her at the window.

"It's not as bad as it was out there earlier," he said contemplatively.

"There's a hooded, insulated jacket in the front hall closet that should fit you. You won't even feel the cold in that baby," Lauren told him.

"All right," Colton agreed, "I'll go put on my shoes and try on that jacket."

"And I'll go get the phone," Lauren said. He watched her walk away, the gentle sway of her hips a thing of beauty.

They met up again at the front hall closet where she helped him into the jacket, reminding him of his mother bundling him up for the cold when he was a child. Then she explained how to use the phone. "It's simple, and it works anywhere in the world, so there shouldn't be a problem reaching your mother."

"How'd you know I wanted to phone my mother?"

"Your father just passed away and you're missing,

whom else would you want to phone? You're not married, are you?"

"No, I've never been that lucky," he said, marveling at how easy it was to talk to her.

She smiled sweetly as she handed him the phone and said, "Tell her my thoughts and prayers are with her."

Lauren had been right, the phone was a cinch to use. He got his mother on the first try. She was sick with worry. "Colton, oh, my God, where are you?"

"I'm in Bryson City, Mom, at the cabin, or rather I'm at your neighbor's cabin. Our cabin didn't have power, so Lauren offered me her guest room."

"That's hours from here," Veronica Riley cried. "And I heard there was a snowstorm expected in that area tonight."

"Blizzard is more like it," Colton said. He looked up at the sky. Stars were starting to peek through the cloud cover. "But things are clearing up. With luck, I'll be home tomorrow."

"Lauren is a sweetheart," Veronica said. "Have you told her about your father?"

"Yes, and she cried," he said, his throat getting full again. "She says her thoughts and prayers are with you."

"Of course they are," said Veronica fondly. "It's not that I'm not glad she was there when you needed her, but why in the world is she up there alone in that godforsaken weather?"

"She told me she wanted to get away from well-meaning people sympathizing with her over her divorce."

"She's divorced?" Veronica sounded startled. "I didn't hear anything about it."

Colton didn't want to go into the nondisclosure clause that Lauren had earlier told him about over the phone. "It was kept quiet," was all he said. A moment of silence passed. "Mom, I'm using a satellite phone under the stars. I'd better go. I'll call you again tomorrow."

"Okay, baby, I'm glad you were able to let us know where you are and that you are safe. You're in good hands," Veronica said confidently.

"Good night, Mom," said Colton with warmth.

"Good night," said Veronica softly.

He'd gone a few yards from the cabin to make his call and now he turned and carefully walked back. The snow came halfway up his legs with each step. He took it slowly, not wanting to fall down in the powder. He'd had enough of the cold for one night.

He guessed Lauren had been watching him from a window because as soon as he reached the cabin, she was there in the doorway, wearing a hooded jacket as if she was ready to come to his rescue should he need her. "Hey, did everything go okay?"

"Yeah, no problem," he assured her.

"Good," said Lauren, "Then get in here. It's freezing!"

Colton was more than glad to oblige. Feeling sure

of his footing, he jauntily put one foot on the bottom step, slipped, lost his balance, and went flailing backward, arms windmilling in an attempt to regain his equilibrium. He wound up on his back in the snow. He was thankful the snow was all he'd landed on.

He found the whole situation ridiculous and started laughing uproariously.

Lauren, in her rubber-soled boots, was off the porch and by his side in a matter of seconds. Laughing, she helped him to his feet and brushed snow off his coat. "Are you all right?"

As they held each other upright, Colton peered into her beautiful face. "No, I haven't been all right all day. My father's gone and I seem to have lost my senses. I drove up here on a whim and ended up unknowingly intruding on your solitude. But now that I've met you and put a personality to the image of you I've seen over the years, I find that I'm strongly attracted to you. I'm definitely not all right."

Lauren's heartbeat accelerated at his admission. "Well, that's normal," she said, her voice warm and gentle. "We're both hurting, needing comfort. And we're here alone. The situation is rife with potential for sexual attraction. I've been checking you out, too."

They took the steps together and made it to the door without another mishap. Inside, Lauren shut the door and they quickly removed their jackets. She then busied herself hanging the damp jackets on the coat tree, appearing to Colton that she wanted to drop the subject.

But he wasn't ready to do that just yet. "And what do you think?"

She looked up at him with big brown eyes and said as innocently as she could muster, "About what?"

Colton smiled. "You know what."

She turned away and began walking toward the back of the cabin. "I think you know you're hot, Colton Riley. How could anyone not? You look in a mirror every day."

"Are you saying I'm conceited?"

"No, I'm saying I'm hot, you're hot, but we should just leave it at that. Any further discussion could lead nowhere good."

"Oh, I think it might lead to somewhere good and something memorable," he contradicted her. "And you think you're hot, too?"

This made her turn to stare at him. "Are you saying I'm not?"

"Hell, no. I think you're smokin' hot. I like the fact that you don't deny it and try, like a lot of women I've met, to fish for compliments. You're confident in your sexuality. I like that."

"Honey, there is nothing wrong with my sexuality. Just because my ex was a cheating bastard doesn't mean I wasn't holding up my end!"

"Touchy subject, huh?" asked Colton. "You don't have to convince me that your ex is a bastard. I don't like him, never have."

"He doesn't like you, either."

There was a calculating light in her eyes that

made him wonder something. "Did he tell you how he cheated me out of several contracts?"

She harrumphed. "I didn't know and didn't want to know anything about his business dealings. And if you think you can get back at him for some dirty deal by sleeping with me, think again. He doesn't care about me. I'm a starter wife, his first wife, but apparently not his last. He's already engaged to number two."

"I don't even think like that," Colton vehemently denied. "My wanting to sleep with you has nothing to do with Adam Eckhart. Does your wanting to sleep with me have anything to do with the fact that he hates me and if it got back to him it might piss him off?"

"No!" Lauren cried.

"Then you do want to sleep with me?"

"Yes, but…"

He moved in. Lauren looked him in the eyes. Her stare was penetrating, as though she could see right through him. He found her scrutiny thrilling and invited it. He had nothing to hide. He wanted her to plumb deep and discover that for herself. He didn't wonder why he was unafraid of being so vulnerable. He just knew she made him grateful to be alive at this moment.

At last, she spoke. "There have to be some ground rules. You don't have a girlfriend, do you?"

"There is no one special in my life," he assured her.

She was looking at him suspiciously. "I won't have a part in another woman getting hurt over infidelity."

"Scout's honor," he said with a straight face.

She seemed to be satisfied with his answer. "Okay, then. What happens here stays here."

"Done," he promised.

"You can't tell anyone."

"Understood," he agreed. "That goes for you, too. Not even your girlfriends."

"Not even your boys," she countered.

"Not even your priest," he said.

"Not even God," she said with a smile.

"I think He already knows," said Colton as he backed her against the wall and planted a sensual, bone-melting kiss on her sweet mouth.

Bodies pressed closer and warmth ensued shortly afterward. By some silent consensus they agreed that this seduction would be slow and deliberate. When they came up for air from that first kiss, their eyes met and they smiled. It was confirmed. They were a good fit. She unbuttoned his shirt, curious to know whether his chest was hairy or smooth. She was rewarded with a hairy, muscular chest and a washboard stomach.

He was patient as she ran her hands over his pectorals and admired his biceps after she had finished removing the shirt. "I like your guns," she said.

"Speaking of guns, you don't keep yours under your pillow, do you? I don't like those kinds of surprises in bed."

She laughed sexily. "No, it's back in the safe. The only thing exploding in my bed tonight will be you."

After that there wasn't very much talk. She took him to her bedroom, which was two doors down from his. When he walked in the room, he saw that her bed had been turned down already, and there was a book on it. She had obviously planned to read until she fell asleep.

He watched as she began removing her clothing piece by piece.

First, her jeans, revealing long, shapely legs and a see-through pair of panties. Then her blouse, under which she wore a lacy cream-colored bra that matched her bikini panties. Her body was lush and feminine yet athletic and she had an ass that a man like him would love to hold in a fit of passion.

After she'd gotten down to her underwear, her gaze fell to his lower half. He unbuttoned the jeans he wore but did not pull them past his hips. "I'm not wearing anything underneath," he warned.

"I'm a grown woman," she told him. "You haven't got anything I haven't seen before."

She removed her bra to make him feel more comfortable. Her breasts were full and everything he desired, not too big, nor too small, just right for palming in his big hands, and the erect nipples were ripe for licking. His mouth watered.

He pulled the waistband of the jeans down past his hips and heard the audible intake of breath from her. He was well-endowed, but not monstrously so. It was nice to know she liked what she saw.

Lauren, suddenly faced with the manifestation of her wanton desire, was having second thoughts. She was pretending to be someone she was not. Adam was the only man she'd ever made love to. She had made it seem to Colton as if she had more experience with men than she actually had. Adam was not nearly as blessed as Colton was when it came to sexual "equipment." She wasn't sure if she could accommodate him.

Too much time had passed with Lauren staring at him for Colton's comfort. "Lauren, is something wrong?"

"No," she denied.

He walked toward her, totally naked, his muscles flexing enticingly, his manhood semi-erect. She couldn't help it. Her body reacted to the sensual image he made. The man was sex personified, and she'd been too long without a lover, a good lover. She was beginning to wonder if Adam had ever been a good lover. After all, she had nothing to compare him to.

There was only one way to find out.

She removed her panties, tremblingly. Colton stopped in his tracks and took all of her in. He sighed with satisfaction. She was not one to mow the lawn, so to speak. She was beautifully natural, which was refreshing as far as he was concerned.

There seemed to be nothing separating them now as he pulled her into his arms, and they fell onto the bed. She molded her body against his. He was fully erect now, and their bodies, his skin a darker cinnamon than hers, wrapped themselves around each other. Their kisses were deep. The taste was like a drug, and her body writhing beneath his worked him into a sexual frenzy.

The smell of her, the silkiness of her skin fed his need. When she opened her legs to him, somewhere in the back of his mind, he remembered condoms. He didn't know if she had any. He hadn't even thought about them until now. But it wouldn't do. No matter how much he wanted her he wouldn't risk getting her pregnant just to satisfy his needs. "Do you have any condoms?" he asked huskily.

"They're in the nightstand drawer," she said with a gesture of her head. He got up and looked in the drawer she'd indicated. Once he had the condom in his hands he tore it open and put it on. He looked back at her to see that she was watching him. He supposed he should feel self-conscious. They were strangers in every sense of the word, especially in a physical sense, but this felt natural.

But he was a man who'd been brought up right. He was a gentleman. So when he pulled her into his arms once more, he looked into her eyes and asked, "Are you sure about this?"

"Yes," she breathed. The expression in her eyes left him no further doubt.

Her willingness pleased him, and his penis grew harder at the thought of penetrating her. But first, her pleasure. He got on his knees and pulled her toward him to the edge of the bed. Her legs were splayed wide, and it was apparent that she was ready for him from the wetness of her sex. He'd been wondering what she tasted like and now he bent his head and devoured her. His tongue moved slowly around her clitoris, inciting a current of electrically charged sensual pleasure throughout her body. She felt it down to her toes. Her moans were low at first and grew louder as her impending orgasm drew nearer.

He left her clitoris and licked the sides of her labia. This made her thighs tremble. She whispered, "Yes, yes, yes..."

Though he was happy she was enjoying his efforts, he wasn't satisfied with that reaction alone. He wouldn't be content until she started calling on a deity. He redoubled his efforts. She rose up on her elbows, "Oh, my God, what are you doing to me?"

He merely smiled.

When she climaxed, she not only released pent-up sexual energy, but she also came to the realization that there was a lot she didn't know about sex, and here was the man who could teach her.

Colton got up and while she was in that malleable state just after an orgasm, when your mind was blown and sensual pleasures were magnified, he entered her. She was just as he imagined she would be—hot, tight and more than capable of handling him.

Never had Lauren had such an enthusiastic, energetic lover, one who seemed to give even more than he got. Her body reveled in it. Felt as if it had been waiting for him all her life. She knew that this feeling was what people were trying to describe when they said that sex was the closest thing to heaven on earth. She'd never felt so alive.

Colton couldn't believe his luck. This woman was

his equal in every way. Not content to lie there and accept his thrusts, she was giving it back to him with as much fervor as he was giving it to her.

When he came it was a monumental moment for him. He didn't know if it was because his emotions were so intense tonight after the day he'd had, or there was something unique about Lauren. She was smiling up at him. She looked exhausted but supremely happy. He was glad he'd had something to do with that.

Chapter 3

"I've done it now," Lauren said jokingly as they lay in bed wrapped in each other's arms. They'd gotten up and showered together and climbed back in bed.

Colton smiled. "What have you done?"

"I've become the Gaines girl who's not only divorced but who, after the divorce, jumped right in bed with the first available man. I left Raleigh to get away from it all and a hunk shows up on my doorstep."

"Life isn't fair," Colton said sympathetically.

Lauren laughed softly. "Darn right, it's not. I was determined to give up men."

He reached out and brushed a tendril of hair behind her left ear. "How long would that have lasted? You're a vital, passionate woman, Lauren. I can tell that much from the little time we've spent together. Don't let Eckhart turn you off men."

"Please don't say that name," said Lauren.

"All right, I'll just say 'the asshole' from now on," Colton said.

"Don't even refer to him at all. I came here to forget he exists."

"Then why'd you come to a place you shared?"

"He was rarely here," Lauren explained. "He bought the place and came a couple of times, met your parents who, as you can imagine, gave him a cool reception. Then after a while, he stopped coming at all. I didn't care. What he didn't know was that I had an ulterior motive when he announced he was buying the property."

"Which was?"

"My granddaddy Beck, my mother's dad, lives up here near the Cherokee reservation. He owns a lodge. I go to see him whenever I come up here. Grandma died about five years ago and he doesn't have any family in the area. My sisters and I make sure one of us goes to see him at least once a month. I was delighted when my ex bought this place. And, thanks to you, I got it in the divorce settlement."

"Thanks to me, how?" Colton wondered.

"Because he got no reaction out of you when we moved across the pond from your place, he lost interest and gave it to me without a fight."

Colton understood. "So when you come up here, it's like going home."

"Exactly," she answered with a contented sigh.

"The only place I'm able to feel that way is my parents' home," Colton told her. "I own a home but it's just a house. A very nice house, mind you, but it has no sentimental value."

"Maybe you haven't been in it long enough," she suggested.

"I bought it six years ago," he replied. He smiled at her. "You're an architect. Maybe you can come take a look at it and tell me what's missing about its design that's preventing me from caring about it."

"That implies that we're going to take this further than this nonreality bubble we're presently in," Lauren warned him.

"Is that what you think is happening here?" Colton asked, the humor gone out of his tone and his eyes. Up until now they had been talking good-naturedly. True, her insistence about keeping this a secret had indicated that she believed this was to be a one-night stand, but after making love he no longer wanted it to be just that. He envisioned seeing her again, slowly getting to know her. He had assumed she felt the same way.

"Wasn't that what we agreed on earlier? That *this* remains our little secret?"

"Yes, Lauren, but I thought you were thinking of your reputation. I didn't believe that you were really going to kick me to the curb afterward. Not if we both enjoyed ourselves. And I know you enjoyed yourself."

"I did *enjoy myself*," she confirmed as she freed her arms from his and sat up in bed. "I simply didn't want to set myself up for disappointment. I wanted you to know that there were no strings."

"Just pleasure," he said as he sat up while maintaining eye contact with her. "I understand not wanting to be hurt, Lauren. Believe it or not, I've been hurt before, too. On the other hand, I don't want you to sell yourself short. Of course I want more than a tryst in the mountains."

"You say that now after sex, but you may feel differently when we get back to Raleigh and to our everyday lives. Plus there's the trauma you are under due to your father's death. People do strange things when they're grieving."

"And you're worried that you might have slept with me just to get your ex out of your system, is that it?" he wanted to know.

Lauren shook her head, but her eyes told a different story. She was undecided. "I'm an emotional wreck right now," she admitted. "I don't know up from down. I only know that I enjoyed being with you tonight."

"That's an honest answer," he said softly as he pulled her back into his arms.

Lauren smiled again as she got comfortable in his embrace. "Let's talk about anything except what might happen after we get back to Raleigh. For instance, how old are you?"

"I'll be thirty-five in October," he easily replied. "And you?"

"I'll be thirty next month."

"How do you feel about that?"

"Same as I felt about twenty-nine—indifferent. I'm not afraid of getting old, I'm just afraid of not accomplishing what I want to in life."

"Which is?"

"To be happy," she simply said.

"What would make you happy?"

"To be successful at what I do," she began. "To have a marriage that is as loving and lasting as my parents' marriage or your parents' marriage, for that matter."

"They did it," Colton reasoned. "I don't see why you can't."

"The world has changed," Lauren said. "What was important to our parents' generation isn't important to ours. Couples get married today knowing there's an easy out. Couples from our parents' generation actually did it believing they were in it for a lifetime."

"I don't agree with that," Colton countered. "I think young people want the same things. We just go about it differently."

"The odds are stacked against us," Lauren said. "Fifty percent of marriages end in divorce."

"Is it that high?" Colton asked incredulously.

"I'm probably quoting old statistics and it's even higher by now," Lauren said.

"You're seeing the world through newly divorced eyes," Colton told her. "Give yourself a few months and you'll see things differently. Now, let's talk Christmas. You know in a matter of minutes, it's going to be Christmas Day. What do you want for Christmas this year?"

"I didn't even bother to get the decorations out of the attic," Lauren said. "I'm not in the Christmas mood this year."

"Humor me," Colton insisted with a coaxing smile.

"Peace on Earth, good will toward men?" Lauren ventured.

"Okay, besides that."

"A warm, sexy man in my bed," Lauren said, grinning at him.

"I think Santa already gave you that, young lady," Colton said and kissed her soundly.

When they broke off their kiss, she asked him what he wanted for Christmas, "For a moment like this to last," was his only reply.

The next morning Colton awakened before Lauren and took the opportunity to observe her while she slept. He could barely hear her breathing, she slept so deeply. She had braided her hair after they'd made love last night for the final time and now it fell in a single tress down her back. She slept on her side and was literally hugging her pillow. He smiled. She looked so young in repose, nowhere near thirty.

He was still watching her when she opened her eyes and smiled at him. "Is it morning already?"

The sun filtered through the sheers at the window. She squeezed her eyes shut against the glare. "Why didn't I put up blackout curtains?"

"You obviously like sunshine in the morning," said Colton as he swung his legs off the bed and stood up. "I have electric shutters in my bedroom that block out everything."

"What are you, a vampire?" she teased.

"If I were, you would be one by now, as well," he told her.

He got down on the floor and began doing push-ups without a stitch of clothing on. Lauren sat up in bed to watch. This was the strangest man she'd ever met. She stopped counting at a hundred.

Climbing out of bed, she said, "I'm exhausted just looking at you. The general would love you. I bet he's out jogging right now."

"I'd love to meet him," Colton said.

But she was gone. He heard the bathroom door close as he switched and began the sit-up portion of his morning regimen.

Momentarily, he heard the sound of Lauren brushing her teeth. After a hundred and twenty sit-ups he got to his feet, gathered his clothing that he'd discarded in the heat of passion last night and went to the guest room to shower and dress.

When he emerged a few minutes later, dressed and ready for his day, whatever it might bring, he heard music and followed the sound to the kitchen where Lauren was cracking eggs into a bowl. She looked up. "There you are. The electricity's back on and the phone's working again but according to Grandpa who knows the guy who drives the snowplow, the roads won't be cleared up here until tomorrow morning. I'm sorry."

Before he said anything, he kissed her good-morning. "Why are you apologizing? You didn't cause the storm."

"I thought you might be worried about your mom being alone at a time like this," she said, concerned.

For a few hours Colton had been able to allow his

mind to rest from the constant assault of grief over his dad's death. Lauren had given him that, and he was grateful to her. But now it all came rushing back. "My sister, Jade, and her family are home from Miami. They're with her," he said.

"Oh, that's good," said Lauren. She turned back around and resumed cracking eggs. "Scrambled eggs and toast all right with you? I don't have any breakfast meats. I'm not a big eater of bacon or sausage and I wasn't expecting guests."

He smiled gently. "Why don't you let me cook for you? You cooked for me last night."

She readily agreed and moved aside to let him take over. He did appear as if he knew his way around the kitchen. He effortlessly whisked the eggs in the bowl and then placed butter in the skillet. At just the right temperature, he added the eggs. He didn't cook them too long, turning off the stove before they congealed, and when he put them on two separate plates they were of a fluffy consistency.

"Where'd you learn that?" Lauren asked.

"The Riley men are all competent in the kitchen," he said. "Grandpa Riley was a chef at a restaurant in New Orleans before he got in his head to come to Raleigh and start a construction business."

"Cooking and building don't seem to go together," Lauren said as she put two slices of bread into the toaster.

"They don't," Colton agreed. "That's only a bit of Riley family trivia."

When the toast was ready, they sat down at the island where Lauren had already put two place settings. She poured orange juice in their glasses. "Coffee?" she asked with the carafe poised over his cup.

"Yes, please," Colton said, smiling at the domesticity of the scene. It was as if they did this all the time. He was very comfortable in her presence.

A local radio station was on in the background. The announcer reported, "That was the worst snowstorm we've had in these parts in years. As our listeners know, we're used to milder winters."

Another voice broke in with "Yeah, Bob, let's hope the temperature doesn't rise too swiftly because if it does we're going to have a muddy mess out there."

"How'd your granddad fare?" Colton asked once music resumed on the radio program.

"He says the lodge is none the worse for wear. That place is built like a fortress," Lauren said fondly.

"He lives alone?"

"Yes, but his business keeps him so busy he isn't lonely. Hunters and fishermen stay there year-round. He has a great staff but I'm afraid at eighty, he's getting a bit old to run the place. I'd never say that to his face because he'd probably bite my head off. He's never going to willingly retire."

"He sounds great," Colton said.

"He is," Lauren was quick to say. "Our mom, Virginia, is his only child. She's been trying to get him to move in with her and the general for years but he says if he and the general lived under the same roof, one of them would wind up shot." She laughed. "He was only slightly exaggerating. He and Daddy don't get along. He never forgave Daddy for marrying his daughter and taking her all over the world. Daddy's been stationed quite a few places and Momma followed him. But then she decided she wanted us to have a more permanent home and that's when they settled on Raleigh. It was a fairly large city and not too far from her father. She got a degree in English and took a job as a teacher and worked her way up to principal. Daddy's retired now, but she's still working and like her own father, shows no signs of retiring anytime soon."

"She sounds like my mom," Colton said. "Only dad's illness got her to slow down. She wanted to spend as much time with him as possible toward the end."

Lauren squeezed his hand in sympathy, but didn't say anything. She always felt that if you didn't know what to say to comfort someone it was best to say nothing at all. Just be there for them.

Colton took a deep, trembling breath. "I feel so helpless. I mean, I'm usually the guy people go to when there's a problem that needs solving. But with this one, I feel totally out of control, unable to cope. It took everything out of me to watch him die in the hospital. Then to see my mother appear to age twenty years right before my eyes after he was gone hit me even harder. Her pain was palpable. I had to get out of there, and I'm sorry to say, I took off. I'll always regret leaving her alone with my sister."

"I'm sure they understand."

"They love me—" he paused "—so they'll say they

understand, but deep down I believe they'll think I abandoned them."

"No, no, please believe me, Colton. Everyone responds differently to the death of a loved one. You had to distance yourself for a while. Your family won't hold that against you."

"Even now," he admitted, "I don't want to go back. I was grateful when you said the roads wouldn't be clear until tomorrow. There's the funeral to plan, the casket to pick out, a suit for dad to wear. I should be doing that. I'm his son."

Since Lauren had known Frank for several years, she felt she could now share with Colton an observation she'd made about his father.

"You're worrying about insignificant things," she said. "The Frank Riley I knew and was very fond of didn't leave matters like his final requests up to chance. He probably left minute details as to exactly how he wanted his memorial service to progress. And even if he didn't, Veronica certainly has in mind how she wants him to be honored. Couples who've been together that long usually have things worked out in advance."

"You think?" Colton was hopeful that she was right because he was at a loss. A big, strong man like him was completely stumped.

"The phones are working," Lauren reminded him. "Phone Veronica after breakfast and ask her."

Colton breathed easier as he finished his breakfast. Lauren had a calming effect on him.

Twenty minutes later he had his mother on the phone.

"Everything's been arranged for some time now," Veronica told him. "Your dad left specific instructions. The only thing I haven't been able to arrange is the New Orleans–style jazz band that'll play him all the way to the cemetery. His words, not mine. Jade's on it. You say you're going to be stuck there another day? Today's Wednesday. The funeral is on Saturday. That's plenty of time for you to get back home."

"I'm so sorry I'm not there with you," Colton told her sincerely.

"I know you are, baby," Veronica said with warmth. "Don't be so hard on yourself. You've always been too hard on yourself. Your father used to wonder if maybe when he was teaching you to run the business he forgot to teach you when to let go. Life isn't all about making money and living up to everyone else's expectations. It's about knowing yourself and knowing when to relax and enjoy the fruits of your labor. You're thirty-four and you haven't fallen in love yet. What's stopping you? Your father and I used to play this game whenever we met a nice young lady. 'She would be perfect for Colton,' I would say, and your father would laugh at me and say, 'Let Colton decide who is perfect for him. Just like I decided you were perfect for me.' That shut me up for a while, but I still wonder whenever I meet a nice woman whether or not she's the one for you," Veronica said with a sigh. Before she said goodbye she reminded him to give her best to Lauren.

Lauren was having her own conversation on the satellite phone as she walked outside on hard-packed snow. Her sister, Amina, a captain in the army who had recently finished a hitch in Afghanistan and was trying to get used to civilian life, was threatening to steal the general's Hummer and come up there and collect her. "It's Christmas," she whined, making Lauren remember when they were kids and Amina, two years younger than herself, began to moan and groan until she wore her down. "No one should be alone on Christmas."

Lauren told her about Colton's unexpected arrival last night.

"It was the damnedest thing. I was in the tub at the time."

Amina screeched with delight on the other end after listening to Lauren's account. "Desiree says he's man-candy. And you know she doesn't say that about just anybody. Is he still there? We're getting in the car now if he is."

"No, you're not," Lauren said with some satisfaction. "The roads aren't fit for driving and won't be until tomorrow."

"Damn!" Amina said disappointedly.

Apparently, Desiree took the phone from Amina because it was her voice that Lauren heard next. "Colton Riley, huh? Women in Raleigh have been trying to trap him for years. He's either very wily or a confirmed bachelor. Be careful. You're very vulnerable right now."

Desiree was a psychotherapist who specialized in

relationships. She had a diagnosis ready for any male her sisters came in contact with. She was so busy solving everyone else's relationship problems she had no time for a relationship of her own.

"You don't have to worry. I just offered him a warm place to stay last night," Lauren said, mindful of the agreement she'd made with Colton. "There's no relationship here for you to analyze, Desi."

The next voice to speak belonged to her sister Meghan. "Hey, sis, don't listen to these two. I hope you're taking advantage of the isolation and getting to know Mr. Riley better."

Lauren smiled at the naughty suggestion coming from Meghan. If any of her sisters could be stereotyped as bookish and a bit of a nerd it would be Meghan who was a history professor.

"It's nothing like that, Meg," she assured her. "He's just the son of my neighbors."

"All right, okay," said Meghan hastily. "I'm just saying that if you let loose and went for it, you're way overdue."

Isn't that the truth, Lauren thought. Her behavior had been exemplary up until now. She could be forgiven for one indiscretion, couldn't she?

Amina was in possession of the phone again. "All right, we won't come up there. But stay in touch and let us know when the roads are clear. We've got to go check on Grandpa. He says he's fine, but he always says that."

"Will do," Lauren promised, "Bye, girls."

She heard them call "Bye!" in unison.

She disconnected and put the phone in the deep pocket of her jacket. Around her the world was snow-covered and looked like a winter scene in a Currier and Ives painting. The pond was frozen over, the tiny dock layered with frost. The oak and pine trees that surrounded the property were snow-laden. They were definitely having a white Christmas.

"Everything okay?" she heard behind her.

Colton had walked out to meet her. She wondered how much of her side of the conversation he'd heard. "Yeah, my sisters threatened to come up here but I told them the roads weren't clear yet."

"You have four sisters, right?"

"Yes, but only three, Desiree, Amina and Meghan, are in the area. Petra's a zoologist studying the Great Apes in Africa."

"No kidding, like Jane Goodall?"

She smiled. There were many facets to him. "Yes, she's been there for over two years now."

"What does she do when she's not studying apes?"

"Actually, she studied to be a veterinarian and worked at a big city zoo before deciding to special-ize and become a zoologist. Now she lectures and has written a couple of successful books on the subject."

"She sounds very accomplished."

"Growing up in our household we were all told to aim high. And even if we didn't hit the mark, we would be giving it our best shot."

"That's a good way of looking at things," Colton said, smiling down at her.

They began walking back to the cabin. "What did Veronica say?" Lauren asked.

"Pretty much what you guessed she'd say," he answered. "They've got it under control. The funeral's on Saturday."

"I'll be there," she said easily. "Unless you don't want me..." She hated that now that they'd been intimate she was wondering if her presence at his father's funeral would make him uncomfortable and perhaps make him relive their time together when he should be focusing on his father. But such were the repercussions of spontaneous sexual relationships. She figured she should expect some awkward moments.

"Please come," he said. His tone was gentle and sure. "I'd like for you to be there and so would Mom."

Chapter 4

"What would you like to do today?" Lauren asked once they were back in the warmth of the cabin.

Colton turned to her with a humorous glint in his eye. "I want to take you on a date."

She laughed shortly as she shrugged off her coat and hung it on the hall tree. "A date, huh? Where are you planning on taking me?"

"A movie, dinner and then, dancing," he said with confidence.

She looked at him as if he'd taken leave of his senses but she was excited by the idea, so she accepted. "What time will you pick me up?" she asked.

"Let's make it six," he said. "I'm eager to get to know more about you."

"What am I supposed to do in the meantime?" she

asked. She had thought they would spend their last day together in bed, like any normal snowbound couple.

"Do whatever you would do if I weren't here," he suggested.

So for the remainder of the day she worked in her office. She devoted a considerable amount of time to making a three-dimensional model of the building she was designing in Raleigh using a program on her computer. It allowed her to see the building from all angles and to visualize it more accurately. At around one o'clock her stomach growled, and she went in search of lunch to find Colton in the kitchen already fixing them sandwiches.

"Hello, Miss Gaines," he said. "You don't mind if I call you, Miss Gaines?"

"Not at all," she said, going to him and planting a kiss on his cheek. She hadn't kissed him since this morning. Colton put down the knife he'd been using to cut the sandwiches in two and pulled her into his arms for a proper kiss.

When he let her go, Lauren was breathless. "Are you sure tonight's our first date? That kiss was kind of fresh if it is. Actually, we should only be shaking hands at this point. And don't even think about getting lucky tonight. Sometimes I don't even kiss a guy good-night on the first date."

When Colton grinned, she noticed he had a dimple in his left cheek but not his right. How could she have missed that up until now? She peered closer. "What happened to your other dimple?"

"A genetic anomaly," he said with a short laugh.

"I'm the third Riley who has only one dimple. What can I say? I'm a freak of nature."

"Another bit of Riley family trivia?"

"I've got a long list." He handed her a smoked turkey sandwich on a plate. "Will you be having your lunch in here with me, or will you be taking it back to work with you?"

"Oh, I'll have it in here with you if I'm not disturbing your date planning," she said with a bit of skepticism.

He let it slide. She may not have confidence in his ability to pull this date off but he was having fun. They sat down at the island and ate their sandwiches. "What kind of movie are we going to see?" Lauren asked after swallowing her first bite.

"Unfortunately, this theater has a shortage of romantic films starring African Americans," he told her regrettably. "However I trust the owner's taste and I'm sure whatever's shown will be worth watching."

Lauren smiled. It was true. She hadn't brought many DVDs with her on her visits to the cabin over the years. Her real collection was at home in Raleigh. "Well, how're you doing on dinner and dancing?"

"The restaurant I'm taking you to has a wonderful menu. You're going to dine on roast chicken, twice-baked potatoes and broccoli in a butter sauce."

"Wow, the chef must be a genius," she quipped. "The last time I visited that restaurant they didn't have roast chicken on the menu."

"Roast chicken, canned chicken, why quibble?"

he asked good-naturedly. "It's going to be a culinary masterpiece."

"If you say so," Lauren said. "And dancing?"

"Ben Harper, Ray Charles and Otis Redding are all appearing at this little club tonight," he told her proudly. "I was able to get reservations."

"How nice of Ray Charles and Otis Redding to make the journey back from the Other Side to entertain us," Lauren said with laughter in her voice.

"I thought so, too," Colton agreed.

Lauren smiled at him. "It sounds wonderful."

Promptly at six that evening, Colton knocked on Lauren's bedroom door. She opened it to find him standing there looking handsome in the clothes he'd first arrived in except he'd freshly laundered them, taken a bath and shaved. He smelled heavenly.

She, too, had paid close attention to her appearance tonight.

She was wearing one of the few dresses she had in her closet: a short sarong-style silk dress in a rich shade of red. It was a summer dress but she figured that didn't matter since they weren't leaving the cabin.

She'd put her hair up and she wore a pair of black sandals with three-inch heels. She'd even applied a bit of makeup for the first time since Colton's arrival. Mascara made her lashes appear longer and the red lipstick gave her mouth a pouty look.

"You're a vision," Colton said appreciatively.

"And you look very handsome tonight."

He offered her his arm. "Shall we?"

She put her arm through his. "Yes, please."

The first thing Lauren noticed as they walked into the living room was that Colton had raided the attic and put up the artificial Christmas tree and decorated it with all her special ornaments. She stood stock-still for a moment, touched by his efforts. She turned to him, her eyes dancing, "It's beautiful."

Colton smiled, warmed by her reaction to the tree. "Merry Christmas, Lauren."

"Merry Christmas," Lauren murmured back, her heart filled with the warmth of the season despite her attempts to block it out.

Colton led her over to the couch and they sat down in front of the TV. He had already put the movie in the DVD player. Now he picked up the remote, and he said, "I hope you haven't seen the new Larenz Tate/ Nia Long movie yet."

Lauren laughed at his description. He'd found a copy of one of her favorite romantic movies. She'd forgotten she owned it.

"No," she said, going along with him. "What's it called?"

"Love Jones," he replied.

Lauren, who'd seen the film at least a dozen times before, thoroughly enjoyed it with Colton. Turned out he had never seen it and initially tagged it a "chick flick." But he admitted, at the end, that it was well executed and dealt with real issues couples faced.

They kissed as the credits rolled. Lauren's lipstick was nearly gone as they'd kissed so much during the movie. She loved the taste of him. Clean, fresh and inviting. Kissing had not been a big part of her life lately. She realized now that she and Adam hadn't shared a memorable kiss for a couple of years before their divorce. She should have known the love had gone out of their marriage when he'd stopped kissing her the way he used to.

Colton looked deeply in her eyes after the kiss ended. He seemed to have sensed a change in her. "What is it? Am I too rough?"

"No," she was quick to reassure him. "I'm enjoying myself. I'm just trying to shake some memories."

He hugged her close. "It's going to take time," he said gently. He frowned. "Was he abusive?"

Lauren didn't answer immediately. Instead, she gave the question some thought. Adam never hit her but he was sometimes verbally abusive. He wanted her to stop working and support him in everything. He said his wife didn't need to work. He was her job. She should be like the wives of other rich men they associated with, women who were content to decorate their houses, attend social functions and look beautiful on their arms. These wives were happy to be at their husbands' beck and call. In return they wore designer clothes, lived in lavish mansions and spent money like it was going out of style. Marriage was a compromise, Adam used to say. And Lauren wasn't willing to compromise. She told him she hadn't spent years in college to simply let her degree gather dust.

She'd been raised to be an independent woman, not to depend on a man for everything. What kind of role model would she be for their future daughters if she were a sycophant with no backbone whatsoever? The subject of children was another bone of contention between them. Lauren wanted them. Adam didn't. He had been raised by a single mother who struggled every day to put food on the table. His no-good father hadn't contributed a cent to him and his two sisters' upkeep. If Lauren had known Adam didn't want children, she wouldn't have married him. There were quite a few revelations he laid on her *after* their wedding. Another was his obsession with youth. He was ten years her senior. She assumed their age difference was enough for him. But he insisted that she dress like someone barely out of their teens. She refused to do that, as well. He wanted her to get breast implants. She believed her breasts were fine just as they were. Nothing she did seemed to please him. Then she found out that at forty he'd found a twenty-two-year-old mistress. That was the last straw. Lauren filed for divorce.

"No," she finally answered Colton. "He wasn't physically abusive, but it became impossible to live with him after a while."

"I know you don't feel comfortable talking about what went on in your marriage, and I'm not going to press you," said Colton. "But I want you to know that if you do feel like you want to talk to me at some later date, I'll be there for you."

He got up and reached for her hand. She smiled at him as he pulled her to her feet and said, "Dinner time, Miss Gaines."

Because they were unable to go out for groceries Colton had improvised with what was in the refrigerator and the pantry. He made a chicken and broccoli stir-fry with canned chicken breast and frozen broccoli seasoned with onions and peppers over a bed of rice. Lauren couldn't figure out how he'd done it, but it was delicious. He'd found half a bottle of white wine in the refrigerator and served the two of them with a flourish.

He sat down across from her. His gray eyes danced with good humor. "My dad used to say it's better to eat a bowl of vegetables with someone you care about than a sumptuous feast with someone you hate."

Lauren squeezed his hand across the table. "You Riley men really do know your way around a kitchen."

"Eat up," Colton coaxed her. "We need to be at the club by nine."

She insisted on washing the dishes while he went into the living room to set up "the club" by moving aside the couch and rolling up the rug that covered most of the hardwood floor.

When she heard Ray Charles's distinctive voice singing, "Night time is the right time…" she went into the living room to find Colton waiting for her with open arms.

Because they didn't want to leave each other's arms they slow-danced their way through Ray Charles's greatest hits, even when the tempo picked up. Her head was on his shoulder, his strong hands on her back, his touch sending delicious sensual currents throughout her body.

She tilted her head up and looked him in the eyes. Should she tell him that he was her first affair? She wanted him to know that this time had been special in case they came to their senses and decided not to see each other again once they returned to Raleigh. No, she told herself. It would make him feel self-conscious. So she didn't say anything. She would let him think she was as sophisticated as he was. This kind of situation was obviously not new to him. He was one of Raleigh's most eligible bachelors, after all.

An upbeat Ben Harper song filled the air and Colton said, "I see you like alternative rock."

"He's not an alternative rocker," Lauren defended her favorite musician.

"Sounds like alternative rock to me," Colton said.

"I'll have you know that Ben Harper is a Renaissance man. He's adept at many styles of music. He's rock, yes, but he's also rhythm and blues. I would follow him anywhere."

"Do I detect a slight crush on Mr. Harper?" Colton asked playfully.

"Maybe," Lauren admitted, equally as playful.

"You're a groupie?"

"I am not," she denied, appalled. "I just buy all of his CDs and go to any of his concerts that are within a hundred miles of Raleigh. But I wouldn't call myself a groupie."

"No, baby, you're definitely a groupie," Colton teased. Then he bent and kissed her forehead. "That's okay, though, I'm not jealous, much. There's one thing I've got going for me that Ben Harper doesn't."

She looked up at him with a challenge in her eyes. "What's that?"

"I'm here," he said simply.

She laughed. "That's a good point."

He placed her hand on his chest. She could feel the steady thud of his heart against his rib cage. "When you touch me my heart sings."

She looked deeply in his eyes. She knew this was only a fantasy. Their emotions were heightened for different reasons but it all added up to the same thing. They were comforting each other in their time of need. That's all it was. Yet, in this moment, it felt so real. In her present emotional state she could see herself loving him forever. That was why complete strangers got married in wedding chapels in Vegas and regretted doing it the next morning, she thought wryly.

She'd abandoned her shoes during the movie and now she had to rise to her tiptoes to kiss him. Colton breathed a satisfied sigh and let her in. He couldn't remember kissing a sweeter mouth. And the things she did with her tongue made him harden in a matter of seconds. He didn't even believe she was aware of her effect on him.

Her eyes were drunk with passion when they surfaced for air. "I want you now," she said. She'd turned into a tigress. Her golden-hued eyes told him in no uncertain terms that he was hers tonight. She would not be denied.

He followed her to the bedroom with his eyes on the sexy sway of her hips in the little red dress she wore. The hem was hitched up high and revealed her long, shapely legs. In the bedroom, she turned to him and unbuttoned his shirt. He let it drift to the floor after it was past his shoulders. Her sultry gaze met his. "Admit it, you knew I was a sure thing tonight," she teased.

"A boy can only hope," Colton breathed. His erection was straining against the confines of his jeans. Lauren noticed the bulge.

She touched him and smiled. "You were a master of self-control today," she complimented him. "As I tried to concentrate on work, all I could think about was making love to you."

"Ditto," Colton assured her.

That was all the small talk they could manage. Colton quickly removed his jeans, briefs and socks. Lauren loosened the folds of her sarong and Colton peeled the dress off her body. She wasn't wearing a bra and had on flesh-colored panties beneath. At first glance she appeared as though she were naked.

Colton kissed her shoulders as he pulled her closer to him. He cupped her breasts, after which he began rubbing her nipples between a thumb and forefinger of each of his hands. Lauren sighed with pleasure and languidly arched her back.

Colton took turns licking each nipple until she felt weak in the knees. She stood in front of him only in her panties. He raised his head, his lips wet from licking her nipples. Sitting on the edge of the bed, he pulled her to him. He kissed her belly, ran his tongue around her belly button and then stuck the tip of his tongue inside, which caused an interesting sensation within Lauren.

When he began pulling down her panties, Lauren

stayed his hand. "Last night, you pleasured me. To-night, I treat you."

"I'm grateful for the offer," he said with a smile, "but the feel of your mouth on me would be more than I could bear right now. Even the thought of that…" He gestured downward with his gaze.

She followed his line of sight. His penis was even harder than it had been earlier.

She took his advice and she let him remove her panties and coax her onto her back on the bed. Colton ran his hands along the insides of her thighs, enjoying the view. Her curly black thatch hid a pink jewel of a clitoris. He bent and sought out the pearl.

Lauren startled at the initial touch of his tongue on her but soon relaxed. A delightful sense of letting go washed over her and then pure sexual pleasure. Honestly, she didn't know whether she was coming or going. It felt so good. Could something that felt this good be wrong?

As his tongue worked its magic, his hands gently massaged her hips, which heightened her experience that much more. His large hands squeezed and squeezed. A sexual explosion spread out from her feminine center to the rest of her. Her thighs trembled with the release, and a satisfied sigh escaped her lips. She was his.

Colton got up and put on a condom. Returning to her, he got on his knees on the bed and straddled her. "Open up for me, baby, and wrap those beautiful legs around me as tightly as you can."

She was a quick study and performed splendidly.

With each thrust his pleasure increased. He felt as though he were climbing higher and higher to heaven. Lauren met each thrust with a push of her own. Her insides quivered. The power within Colton was transferred to her and for one incredible moment they were in sync. She once again scaled the peak and met him up there. They collided and sparks flew. As they came down together, their pelvises pressed so close together they could have melded in the heat of the moment, all she could think was, if this wasn't love, she didn't know what was. And that was the crux of the problem. The reason she was up here in the first place was because she hadn't known what love was and had married the wrong man.

She could not make the same mistake twice. That was why she knew that once she and Colton were back in Raleigh, she would not seek him out. She had to get her head straight first.

Colton, on the other hand, knew that he wanted to see her again, and as often as possible. He had never met a woman quite like her. He would pursue her with every ounce of his being.

Chapter 5

The next morning they didn't make a big production out of saying goodbye. They made love upon awakening, showered separately, dressed and had a quick breakfast. Then Colton walked across to his family's cabin to make sure the storm hadn't caused any damage. Satisfied, he returned to Lauren's place. They did think to exchange business cards, and each of them quickly scribbled their personal cell phone numbers on the backs of them.

He got into his SUV and Lauren leaned in and briefly kissed his lips. "Safe trip," she said warmly. "I'll see you on Saturday." She had made a promise and she intended to keep it.

"I'll look forward to it," he replied lightly.

He put the car in gear and drove off. Earlier that

morning the snowplow owner had been true to his word and now the roads were navigable.

Lauren stood and watched the SUV all the way to the county road turnoff. Then she went inside. She would be leaving shortly herself. Before returning to Raleigh, though, she would check up on Grandpa Beck.

"What were you thinking heading to the mountains when you knew they were expecting a snowstorm?" Virginia Beck-Gaines cried when she saw her daughter later that evening. "I was worried sick about you!"

"I found out about the storm after I got there and I only came by here to give you an update on Grandpa," Lauren said irritably. She and her mother were known to butt heads, but she was in no mood to get into it right now. She was tired from her trip. They were in the big kitchen of her parents' five-bedroom house on the outskirts of Raleigh. The house sat on ten acres of land. Their closest neighbor was half a mile away. They liked their privacy.

Virginia, called Ginny by her husband, was short and slender. Anyone who knew her joked that she stayed too busy to gain weight.

She wore her long black hair with silver streaks in a twist at the back of her neck. Her caramel-colored skin was wrinkle-free except for the beginnings of crow's feet. Half African American and half Cherokee, she had the high-cheekbones of her ancestors. Her daughters had inherited her bountiful hair and their various shades of brown skin were crosses between their mother's golden brown skin and father's darker brown shade.

Her size belied her strength and her influence on her family. There was no doubt that she ruled the roost, even though the rooster was six-four and over two hundred pounds.

"Ginny, would you let the girl get a word in edge-wise?" Lauren's father asked in her defense. "She's safe and sound and that's all that counts." He regarded Lauren. "How is the old reprobate?"

Retired general Alfonse "Fonzi" Gaines had been trying to ignore them by concentrating on his cross-word puzzle, but no such luck. Fonzi was completely bald. He'd been shaving his head since his mid-forties when his hairline started receding. A disciplined ex-soldier, he jogged each morning. He had a weakness for his wife's cooking so he had to stay active in order to maintain his trim physique.

"He's fine," Lauren answered gratefully. "He's got a family of twelve up there celebrating Christmas at the lodge. They're from Florida. He says they were thrilled with all the snow. He had to nearly tie them down to keep them from going skiing the next day, but he explained that if anyone got lost out there they would freeze to death before rescue workers could get to them due to the road closures. That took the wind out of their sails."

"What is this I hear about your having a guest for the past two days?" Ginny wanted to know.

Lauren had expected an interrogation. She wished she had sworn her sisters to secrecy. She calmly gave her parents the tame version of Colton's visit. And the reason he'd dropped in.

Ginny had a concerned expression on her face after Lauren had finished relating the tale. "I did read in the paper that Frank Riley had passed away. He was well respected in this town. I'm sure there'll be a huge turnout for his funeral."

On Saturday, Lauren arrived early for the memorial service with her sister Desiree, who had insisted on accompanying her. The two of them found a parking space as close to the church as they could get, which happened to be on the street because the church's parking lot was already packed. On West Edenton Street, St. Paul AME Church was the oldest African American church in Raleigh. Inside, the pews were as packed as the parking lot. Lauren and Desiree, both wearing dark, tailored skirt suits, were able to squeeze into a pew in the middle of the church. Shortly after they were seated the choir began to sing a mournful spiritual.

Lauren strained to see if she could catch a glimpse of the family on the front pew, but she couldn't see much. Women's stylish hats blocked her view. She noticed the casket was closed and there was a poster-size photograph of Frank on an easel to the side of it. It was not a recent photo and she could easily see Colton's resemblance to his father. They had the same color eyes and the same square shape to their jaw.

An usher had given her a program when she'd walked through the door and she read it now. She saw that Frank had been the eldest son in a family of four children. He was survived by a sister and two brothers. He and Veronica had had two children, Franklyn Colton Riley, Jr., and Jade Veronique Everett. Jade had given them two grandchildren.

Looking around the ornately decorative church that had been built in the Late Gothic Revival architectural style, Lauren noted several town officials, including the mayor in attendance.

The stained-glass windows caught her attention momentarily. Bright sunshine streaming through gave the colors in them a kaleidoscopic effect. After the choir finished its selection, a minister took the pulpit and offered a prayer. Lauren's heartbeat quickened when the minister sat down, and Colton walked onto the stage and began the eulogy. He had not mentioned he would be doing the eulogy. But then perhaps he'd been encouraged to do it after he'd gotten back home.

He was a natural. At first his voice trembled slightly with emotion, but he soon got hold of himself and he went on to speak reverentially about his father. "Like most sons," he said, "I resented my father giving me advice on how to live my life. I thought his suggestions were old-fashioned and were designed to ensure I would follow in his footsteps. Thinking I knew better than he did, I didn't listen to his advice. I made my own decisions.

"Those of you who know me are aware that I went through a period of time when I wanted to party 24/7. I worked in the family business, yes, but my heart wasn't in it. I worked from Monday to Friday but at quitting time I was ready to have a good time. And Saturday and Sunday, I didn't go to church—those were my days to really cut loose. I drank too much and I lost count of the number of women I went through. Seeing I was wasting my life, my dad pulled me aside and said, 'Son, what do you value most?'

"I gave him some insincere answer about valuing family. He laughed at me and told me that if I truly valued family I would be doing everything in my power to make sure that when the time came I would be ready to take the reins of Riley Construction instead of slowly killing my body with alcohol and my soul with womanizing. Of course, I didn't listen. I didn't get it until he told me he was dying. Then, I was slapped in the face with reality and I knew he'd been right. If I cared about my family I would be preparing myself to pick up where he left off. I still drink but I don't do it excessively. I've learned what moderation means. And I respect women. I've become the man my family needs, but it was at a terrible expense. My father's gone. I miss you, Dad."

She'd been wrong. It wasn't a eulogy Colton had given. It had been a personal goodbye to his father. Not the story of his father's life, but the story of a son's redemption.

There were tears in her eyes when he finished.

It was Frank's eldest brother, Tad, who gave the eulogy after Colton sat down. By the end of the service Lauren and several people around her had shed plenty of tears.

When they stood to watch the casket being carried

out by the pallbearers, she whispered to Desiree, "I know I told you I wouldn't be going to the cemetery but I changed my mind. Will you be okay getting a taxi home?"

Desiree, who had said earlier she didn't want to go to the cemetery because those places gave her the creeps, now relented. "I'm not going to desert you. I can see how emotional you got after Colton's speech. It's almost as if you care about him."

"I'm not the only person here who found what he said touching," Lauren pointed out. She realized Desiree was not being mean-spirited but she wished just once her brainy sister would not be compelled to voice her opinions.

They fell silent until the procession with Frank's body had passed. Then they filed out of the church with the more than five hundred other people who had come to pay their respects.

Outside, Lauren took a deep, cleansing breath and carefully made her way through the throng of people who were milling about chatting instead of making their way to their cars to follow the hearse to the cemetery.

She looked around to see if she'd lost Desiree in the crowd. But she soon saw that her sister had been waylaid by a tall, broad-shouldered man in an expensively cut black suit.

As she stood there debating whether or not to go back for Desiree, a voice from behind said, "I thought I spotted you."

She turned at the sound of Colton's voice and her

stomach muscles constricted painfully at the sight of him. He was dressed impeccably in a black suit, crisp white shirt and burgundy silk tie with highly polished wingtips on his feet. But his face was tired and drawn. Her heart went out to him.

She wrapped her arms around him when he came in for a hug. He squeezed her tightly and spoke hurriedly. "We're heading to the cemetery now, but I'd love it if you'd come to the house." He slipped a card in the palm of her hand. "Here's the address." He looked in Desiree's direction. "Is that one of your sisters?"

"Yes. Desiree," she said.

"Don't worry about her. That's my cousin Decker with her." He pecked her on the cheek. "I've got to go. They're waiting on me in the limousine. You will come?"

"Yes," she found herself saying even though she didn't think it would be a wise thing to do. Already her emotions were betraying her. Instead of reacting mildly to his presence after not seeing him for twenty-four hours, she had been ridiculously glad to see him.

He jogged away as soon she acquiesced. As he climbed in the back of the limousine he smiled at her and gave her a little wave. Desiree caught up with her a few minutes later after having finally shaken Colton's cousin.

"Oh, my God," she complained, her voice low, "I can't believe I've just been hit on at a funeral. He's a prime cut of man-beef. But really, this isn't a typical pickup venue."

Lauren laughed softly. "That was Colton's cousin Decker."

Desiree flashed a business card. "Mr. Decker Riley, Esq.," she read. "Shakespeare had it right when he wrote, first kill all the lawyers. Mr. Riley's really full of himself."

"I'm sorry you feel that way because my plans have changed," Lauren told her regrettably. "We're not going to the cemetery after all. We're going to the Rileys' home."

They began walking toward the street where Lauren had parked the car. The crowd had thinned somewhat so the path was clear. Desiree, a bit shorter than her long-legged older sister, had to nearly run to keep pace. "I kind of feel like the best friend in a romantic comedy," she said a bit breathlessly. "First you told me you were going to the funeral because you were friends with Frank and Veronica Riley and it was only right to show up to pay your respects. Then you tell me you're extending your respects by going to the cemetery. Now you tell me you're getting in even deeper by going to the Rileys' home."

When they were nearly there Lauren remotely unlocked the doors. "I'll explain on the drive over," she promised.

The black late-model Range Rover wound its way through traffic as they traversed downtown Raleigh and turned and headed out of town to the suburbs.

"What's going on, Lauren?" Desiree asked. "While I was talking to God's gift to women, I looked back and saw you hugging Colton as though you two hadn't seen each other in years. That's not how people act who have just met and are casual acquaintances."

"I'm emotionally raw," Lauren admitted. "Maybe I'm experiencing what people say happens when you save somebody's life. I feel responsible for him now."

"You're getting way too attached," Desiree said, stating her opinion once more. "You did what any decent human being would have done. You let him in out of the cold, nothing more." Her eyes narrowed, her expression grew contemplative. "Or, is there something you're not telling me?"

"If I were keeping a secret, do you think that question would get it out of me?"

"Then something did happen between you two when you were snowed in!" Desiree exclaimed triumphantly.

"Really, Desi, you should learn to curb your imagination. I simply like the Rileys, both Veronica and Colton. I've known Veronica for more than three years. I've just met Colton, but he seems like a decent man. A man who reminds me of his father, whom I enjoyed knowing."

"Oh, please," said Desiree sarcastically. "You're backpedaling so fast smoke is coming out of your ears. You like Colton Riley like I like chocolate and you know I love the stuff. I would marry it if it were possible."

Smiling, Lauren said, "You and most of the women in the world. Seriously, I'm not in love with Colton Riley."

"Then you're in lust with him," said her very wise sister.

Lauren didn't deny it. "Should I make an appointment with you to talk about it?"

"That depends," said Desiree. "Is he in lust with you, too?"

"I would say yes," Lauren said confidently.

Desiree sighed deeply. "I can see now that all my earlier warnings came too late. But you know what? Your falling off your pedestal has been a long time coming. You were a virgin when you married Eckhart and I'm sure you never cheated on him, even though you probably had plenty of provocation."

"Could you speak plain English on occasion?" Lauren asked. "I know you're the brain in the family, but give us poor average people a break."

"You're not that average," said her sister sweetly. "Anyway, what I'm saying is, so what? You had a fling with Colton. It's nothing to get all guilty and repentant over. You're both free agents. Wait, he isn't involved with anyone, right?"

"He told me he isn't," Lauren confirmed.

"Okay, then," Desiree continued, "my only concern is that you're newly divorced and have probably not gotten over the hurt yet. Although, I don't see why you don't recognize the fact you're well rid of that snake."

"I'm realizing it more every day."

"Good. So, I'm just worried that you got it on with Colton because you wanted to test whether or not you were still desirable and Colton got it on with you because he was distraught over his father's death and found comfort in your bed. Other than that, I say go for it."

Lauren laughed shortly. "You hit the nail on the head. Should I keep seeing him for the hot sex, or cut my losses because a relationship based on a fling has no future?"

"It was hot, huh?" Desiree asked, observing her sister's face. Lauren couldn't hide the longing expression that fleetingly crossed her face.

"Honestly, the best I ever had," Lauren said.

"Well, come on now," said her sister, throwing cold water on that statement. "You've only had two men so far. I've had more lovers."

"Interesting," said Lauren. "Care to tell me how many more lovers you've had?"

"Four more," Desiree answered nonchalantly. "A couple of them weren't worth the effort. Bad is an understatement to describe their performances in bed. I'm not saying you can't have great sex without being in love, but my best experiences were with Noel, and I loved that man more than chocolate."

Lauren sighed sadly in sympathy for her sister's loss. Noel Alexander had died tragically in a boating accident during Desiree's senior year of college. They had been engaged.

"So from personal experience, I think what you're feeling for Colton might be more than mere lust. Perhaps you made a personal connection. The only way to find out is to let this play out. To do that you'll have to risk getting hurt again. Are you willing to risk it?" Desiree asked.

Lauren didn't answer immediately. She knew Desiree expected her to give it some thought. Her first instinct was to guard her heart and oftentimes her first instinct had turned out to be the wisest choice. But Desiree had been right when she said it was about time Lauren fell from her self-imposed pedestal. It was time she took some risks.

No one accomplished great things without some risk. "I think it's worth it," she finally said. "What if he's the one for me in spite of the unusual way we met?"

Desiree seemed pleased with her decision "I can't wait to tell Mina and Meg," she said with a big smile.

"You can't tell anyone else," Lauren said hurriedly. "Colton and I promised each other that our affair would be just that, our affair. Aren't therapists supposed to keep what patients tell them confidential?"

"You're not my patient. You're my sister," Desiree pointed out. It was apparent she was eager to share what she'd learned with Amina and Meghan. "I won't breathe a word of it to Mom and Dad, but you've got to let me tell the girls."

"No, Desi." Lauren wouldn't budge.

"Then you'd better give me a dollar," Desiree caved in.

"Why should I give you a dollar?" Lauren asked.

"Payment for my services," Desiree said. "I consider what I do to be as important as what lawyers do. Legally, you're not my patient until there has been an exchange of legal tender for my expertise."

Busy driving, Lauren briefly glanced at her sister to see if her expression was serious. It was. "Oh, okay, look in my purse and get a dollar. But I want a receipt!"

Chapter 6

The Rileys' sprawling three-story antebellum-inspired house sat on a hundred acres of verdant land near a lake. Ancient oak trees with branches covered in moss dotted the property. It was the picture of genteel Southern living.

Lauren guessed this was a gathering exclusively for family and close friends because when she and Desiree arrived there were only about thirty cars parked in the circular driveway.

The housekeeper greeted them at the door and directed them to the solarium where waitstaff carrying trays of canapés circulated among the guests. A bar was set up in the corner of the room.

"They certainly have class," Desiree whispered.

"Lauren!"

Lauren heard her name being called from across the room and looked up to find Veronica heading their way. In her late fifties, Veronica was tastefully dressed in a black sleeveless A-line sheath with a matching jacket and black pumps. Her shoulder-length dark-brown hair had gold highlights that brought out the gold in her eyes. Lauren was enveloped in her arms. She fondly pressed her cheek to hers and then released her to get a good look at her. "I was glad when Colton told me he'd invited you. It gives me the chance to thank you for what you did for him. Thank you, dear."

Lauren smiled shyly. "There's no need for thanks, Veronica. He was the perfect houseguest. He cooked and did his own laundry." Lauren thought it best to keep things light. The day had probably been unbearably sad for Veronica.

Veronica laughed softly as she took notice of Desiree for the first time. "This must be Desiree. It's a pleasure to meet you."

"The pleasure's all mine," Desiree said sincerely.

She and Desiree clasped hands briefly, and Veronica looked at the sisters side by side. "There's a strong resemblance," she said. "There are five of you altogether, right?"

"Yes," Lauren answered, "Although only four of us live in the area."

"Ah, yes, one of your sisters is studying the Great Apes in Africa."

"I'm afraid I tell my mom everything," Colton said

as he joined them. "But I didn't know she actually listened to me."

He offered Desiree his hand. "It's wonderful to meet you, Desiree."

Desiree firmly shook his hand and smiled up at him. "Likewise, Colton," she said. "I'm so sorry for your loss."

"Thank you," he said simply. Then he turned to Lauren, and said, "I have something to show you." He looked apologetically at Desiree. "You don't mind if I steal her for a few minutes, do you?"

Desiree was magnanimous. "Of course not. Keep her as long as you like. I was getting tired of her anyway."

Lauren quickly cut her eyes at Desiree before turning to follow Colton.

In Colton and Lauren's absence, Veronica moved closer to Desiree. "I don't know about you but I'm famished. Would you join me for something to eat?"

"Sure," said Desiree and she followed Veronica out of the solarium to the kitchen.

"The staff is circulating with finger foods," Veronica explained, "but who can satisfy their hunger on that stuff?"

Desiree found Veronica Riley was a woman after her own heart.

She'd missed breakfast that morning and the array of Southern dishes displayed on the huge island in the center of the kitchen made her mouth water. She was putting a slice of juicy ham on her plate right next to a serving of potato salad when Decker Riley strode into the room. "Auntie, I've been looking everywhere for you. The pastor has to leave and he wanted to speak with you about something before he left." He stopped in his tracks when he spotted Desiree and smiled broadly. "We meet again," he said, the delight evident in his deep baritone.

Veronica was chewing a mouthful of collard greens and cornbread. She swallowed. "Child, tell the pastor to come back here. I'm not leaving this kitchen until I'm full as a tick. Desiree will be here when you get back. Won't you, Desiree?"

Desiree smiled politely. "I'm not going anywhere."

Decker reluctantly spun on his heels and went to give the pastor his aunt's message.

Veronica smiled at Desiree. "He comes off a bit too strong but he's really a decent young man."

Desiree had good instincts about people and she believed Veronica Riley was the type of woman who saw things clearly and consequently spoke her mind. "We met earlier at the church and 'player' was the first impression I got."

Veronica sighed. "I don't know why young men these days think that image appeals to women. I think it turns off more women than it attracts. I feel that some so-called players are really insecure. It seems to be all a facade they hide behind in order to protect themselves from getting hurt."

"You're very perceptive," Desiree told her. "That's *my* theory, as well."

Veronica smiled. "I knew when I met you that we were two of a kind."

* * *

When Colton had said he had something to show Lauren, he hadn't been using that as an excuse to get her alone. He really did have something to show her. However, they had to run an obstacle course to get where he was taking her. His dad's study.

They were stopped by his sister, Jade, as he and Lauren began climbing the stairs to the second floor. Lauren found Jade to be as charming as her mother and brother. She was tall and full-figured. Her skin was dark chocolate like her father's and she had jewel-like golden-brown eyes that sparkled with happiness. Her husband, Manu Everett, who was half Samoan and half African American, was a couple inches taller than Colton's six-two frame, but he was about the size of a refrigerator.

"Colton, is this Lauren?" Jade asked excitedly.

Colton introduced them. Lauren couldn't help smiling. Jade's face was so animated. *How does she manage to look this happy,* Lauren wondered, *when they just buried their father today?*

That was when Manu walked up, grinning, and greeted them. He had the same light of natural happiness in his eyes. He playfully picked up his wife from behind and set her back down on the floor. "Hey, everybody," he said warmly.

"Manu," Jade said, "This is Lauren, the woman who saved my crazy brother's life."

Manu's face broke into an even wider grin. "We're indebted to you, Lauren. I don't know what we'd do if something happened to this dude." He playfully punched his brother-in-law on the arm. Lauren knew from Colton's wince that it had hurt.

"He was actually company for me," Lauren graciously said. "Without him I would've been trapped in a blizzard all by myself."

"I hope he was a good houseguest and didn't leave his wet towels on the bathroom floor," Jade joked.

Lauren looked up at Colton in mock horror. "You don't really do that, do you?"

"I have no idea what Jade is talking about," Colton denied. "Now, if you two will excuse us, Lauren and I have something to discuss in private."

Manu hugged his wife. "Well, go on, my brother. No one's stopping you."

"Mommy, Daddy!" Two adorable children, a boy of about six and a girl of about three came running up to them.

Manu grabbed both of them to either side of him with powerful arms. "Didn't I tell you to stop running?"

In that instant, Lauren had her answer to how Jade managed to look so happy on such a sad day. She had love in abundance.

Lauren was delighted to be introduced to Colton's niece and nephew, and then Colton took her firmly by the hand and led her upstairs.

Colton stuck his head in the room to make sure that no one else had sought a bit of peace and quiet in his dad's study before ushering Lauren inside the bookshelf-lined room.

Elegant, yet homey, the room reflected its late owner's tastes. A huge cherrywood desk sat atop a Persian rug in front of a bay window. There was the faint scent of a sweet variety of tobacco in the air. Leather sofas faced each other with a large square coffee table between them. Frank's antique chess set was the only thing on the tabletop.

Lauren remembered it fondly. She used to joke with him that she hoped the elephants whose ivory the chess pieces had been carved out of had died of natural causes. Frank had found that hilarious. "And I suppose that chicken you're eating committed suicide?"

A dark brown leather Queen Anne chair sat near the fireplace, a reading lamp next to it. A red wool throw was on back of the chair. It looked so inviting that Lauren couldn't help but sit in it, her mind on its previous owner. She looked around admiringly. Frank had left an indelible imprint on this room.

Colton locked the door behind them so they wouldn't be disturbed without advance warning.

Lauren noticed his actions and smiled, but she didn't move from her seat. She hadn't come here today to find an empty room and make out with Colton. She'd come to show support. As always, though, her body betrayed her loftier intentions. She wanted to kiss him, and deeply.

To mask her desires, she started talking. "What you said today was very touching."

"It was the truth," Colton said as he slowly walked toward her. "I've worked hard to change. But I'm far from perfect. I'm always discovering something I need to work on. What I've discovered lately is that I have the capacity for becoming one of those annoying people who is completely obsessed with someone else. So obsessed that they think about them all the time, crave their touch and even dream about them."

As he said this and walked toward her, he held her captive with his mesmerizing gaze. His gray eyes were dark and stormy and so damned sexy. Her body, it seemed, rose from the chair of its own accord. She fairly floated into his arms. And the kissing began.

They moaned with the sheer pleasure of their mouths finally being able to come together in this common but astonishing manner. Colton had read somewhere that kissing raised levels of neurotransmitters like dopamine and serotonin. They made you feel happy and horny and that was what made kissing such an enjoyable act. He was a man of nearly thirty-five years old and he didn't remember ever getting such a thrill from kissing as he did when he engaged in it with Lauren. She was beautiful, yes. But he'd dated many beautiful women. So what *was* it about her?

"We're back in Raleigh," he said softly, "And I, for one, don't want to forget what happened between us. I want to date you, in public. That's my decision."

Lauren went with her heart. "I'm in total agreement."

Colton grinned. "Great, because I need a date for the Black and White Ball."

"That's on New Year's Eve," said Lauren in a near panic. Last year, she'd gone with Adam and it had been one of the worst experiences of her life. The ball was attended by premier businesspeople in Raleigh. The attendance fee was a grand and most of the proceeds went to local charities. To Lauren, that was the only reason to participate. However, Adam attended to network and to be seen. Last year's event had certainly been memorable, to say the least.

"My marriage crashed and burned at the ball last year," Lauren told Colton.

His brows arched questioningly. "I remember seeing you there. You looked exquisite. You were smiling as if there was nowhere you'd rather be."

"I became very good at pretending the last year of our marriage," Lauren said sadly. "Do you want to hear what happened or not?"

Colton had been holding her by her arms. He let go of her and gestured to one of the couches.

"No, thanks," Lauren said. "I'd rather stand for this."

She could still see the scene that had unfolded in the ladies' room the night of the ball. She had used the facilities and emerged from the stall to wash her hands and check the state of her makeup only to be accosted by a young woman in a white gown. The women in attendance wore either a black gown or a white gown. She'd worn white that night, as well. Her gown had been a Grecian-inspired one-shoulder creation. The other woman wore one with a plunging neckline and a side-slit almost up to her waist. She had curves in all the right places and meant for them to be seen.

A redhead, her skin was the color of toasted almonds and her eyes were blue. Lauren remembered thinking she must not be a real redhead because redheads generally had paler skin, not brown skin. At any rate, she could have given a supermodel a run for her money. "You're Mrs. Adam Eckhart, aren't you?" she asked Lauren. Her tone had been friendly and admiring. Lauren's guard was down because this wasn't the first time a young woman had approached her to try and get in her good graces. Adam Eckhart was a rich, powerful man and it could be to a young woman's advantage to get in good with his wife. It got you closer to the great man himself. And if you failed to get to him, at least you would be in his orbit and there were other successful men who ran in his circles who were worth latching on to.

Lauren wrongly assumed the redhead was one of these women.

"Yes," she'd replied, equally friendly. "I am, and you are?"

They were standing in the middle of the ladies' room, other women moving around them. The redhead looked Lauren straight in the eye, her stare unflinching. "My name is Joy Summers and I'm his mistress."

She hadn't even lowered her voice, just said it out loud for everyone to hear. Several women gasped and immediately turned to stare at this vulgar young woman who'd chosen to confront her lover's wife at the social event of the season.

Lauren felt sick to her stomach. She'd suspected Adam was cheating but suspecting it and having proof of it were two entirely different things.

She recovered fairly quickly, though. Years of inculcation by her mother and father to always be poised and behave intelligently in public came to her rescue. She met the redhead's challenging gaze, and said, "And what does that have to do with me?"

The redhead's eyes bugged out. She had not expected such a response. "I thought you'd want to know."

The other five women in the room showed no signs of leaving. They stood rapt, hanging on every word. Lauren calmly said, "I already knew, thank you. Is there anything else you'd like to say? For instance, you're sorry for not telling a married man to go to hell when he first hit on you? Because you must have known Adam Eckhart was married. Or do you specialize in married men?"

"Don't kill the messenger," said the woman, smiling as though she'd exacted a coup with that comeback.

One of the onlookers sniffed derisively. "If it was me I'd do more than kill you."

Lauren looked sharply at the woman. "I've got this."

"Handle it, sister," encouraged the woman.

"Obviously you feel confident in your status as his mistress," Lauren said, "Or you wouldn't risk his wrath. Married men like keeping their affairs quiet. That's the point of an affair. It's a naughty delight. It loses its appeal after it's been revealed." She circled the woman much like a lioness checking out her prey before pouncing. "Maybe you think I'll divorce him and then he'll come running to you. I've never heard of that happening but you might get lucky. Who knows?"

"I'm pregnant with his child," the redhead tossed out as her trump card.

"Then that's why you've come here with this desperate attempt to win a permanent place in his life," Lauren surmised. With that, she turned to leave.

"I'm sorry for everything," the redhead shouted at her retreating back. "I had no alternative but to show up here and embarrass him into taking responsibility."

"Good luck with that," Lauren had called back.

"She really was his mistress," Lauren said to Colton now. "But that stunt she pulled was the end of her. Adam dropped her soon after. He's engaged to someone else now. I have no idea if there was ever really a baby involved."

Colton hugged her close. "Forget the Black and White Ball then. We'll ring in the new year together anywhere you want."

Concerned by his state of mind so soon after his father's death, Lauren asked while looking him in the eyes, "Are you sure you're up for a celebration?"

"Dad wouldn't have had it any other way," Colton assured her. "For years the Black and White Ball has been the big blowout of the year for the company. We make generous donations to local charities. It made Dad feel like Santa Claus at the end of the year."

"All right," she relented, noticing the look of pride on Colton's face. "I'll go with you."

"But what about your bad memories from last year's ball?"

"I'm no longer married to that cheater," she reasoned. "I doubt I'll be cornered in the ladies' room by one of his mistresses again."

Colton hugged her tightly. "I'm going to make sure you have a good time. Now, for what I wanted to show you."

Lauren's brows arched in surprise. "You mean you really did have something you wanted to show me? I thought that was a ploy to get me alone."

"Only partly," Colton said, releasing her and walking over to his father's desk. He opened a drawer and withdrew an envelope and walked back over to Lauren and handed it to her.

Puzzled, Lauren looked down at the envelope, which was made out of expensive vellum paper in a rich cream shade. Her name was scrawled on it in cursive.

"It's from Dad," Colton said.

Tears sprang to Lauren's eyes at the thought of Frank thinking enough of her to leave her a personal message. She eagerly opened the envelope and read the enclosed note aloud, "Lauren, I want you to have my chess set because you and I spent wonderful evenings both challenging and getting to know one another. If I'd had a second daughter I would want her to be just like you. By the way, I inquired and the pieces were made from the ivory of an elephant by the name of Hannibal. He spent his last days at a retirement home for elephants in Botswana where he died in his sleep. Being an environmentalist himself, I'm sure Hannibal wouldn't mind your having a part of him. Frank."

Lauren cried even harder after reading his message. Colton pulled her into his arms.

He bent and kissed her, tasting her tears. "Stop crying now. Dad didn't want anyone crying over him. You know what he wrote in his letter to me? He said, 'Colton, I can't tell you how to remember me. You'll have formed your own opinion of me over the years. But I hope you'll remember that I liked to laugh and I worked hard. I loved your mother and you and your sister and when I made friends I kept them for life. I don't want you to waste a minute of your life. Don't cry for me. Be happy that I knew how to have a good time while the getting was good. I wish you happiness, son.'"

"That's so sweet," Lauren said.

Colton laughed. "Only you and my mother would describe Dad as being sweet. He was a tough SOB, but he was fair and honest and he loved his family. He was a good man. The kind of man I aspire to be one day."

"You're already a good man, Colton Riley."

Someone knocked on the door. Colton shot an irritated look in its direction and reluctantly released Lauren to open the door.

Veronica stood on the other side. "Um, hi. Wouldn't you and Lauren like to come downstairs and join us? There's food in the kitchen. You two must be ravenous by now."

Colton immediately knew he'd been tattled on by his sister or perhaps his brother-in-law. Both were equally immature and loved playing practical jokes on him. They'd probably told his mother he'd taken

Lauren upstairs with seduction in mind. True, he'd wanted to steal a kiss, but he'd never make love to Lauren and risk embarrassing her in a house full of people on the day of his father's funeral.

He looked back at Lauren and laughed. "Shall we go down before all the potato salad's gone?"

Lauren wiped her tears away and smiled. "I am a little hungry."

She noticed Veronica was observing her closely as they started downstairs. "Have you been crying, dear?"

"I gave her the letter Dad left for her," Colton explained.

"I see," said Veronica sympathetically. She pulled Lauren into the crook of her arm and held her close to her side all the way downstairs. "I helped him write the letters. He was in good spirits the day he wrote yours. He smiled the whole time and when he finished, he said he knew you'd get a kick out of that."

"He was right," Lauren assured her. Taking Colton's advice that Frank didn't want anyone crying over him, she took a deep breath and smiled.

Chapter 7

Lauren was pleased to return to work on Monday. Work centered her. Her current commission was to design the new children's hospital. She'd been with the architectural firm of Lawrence, Mayer and McGill since she was twenty-two. She had interned there and the senior partner, Albert Lawrence, had liked her so much he'd offered her a permanent position after she'd graduated from Duke University. For some time family and friends had encouraged Lauren to start her own firm. But she enjoyed being part of a design team. She also liked being able to concentrate fully on her work and not have to worry about renting an office space, hiring reliable staff and all the other hassles of running your own firm. Maybe one day, she had thought.

When Lauren stepped off the elevator, she greeted

the firm's receptionist, Meredith, a stout middle-aged black woman who wore her long gray hair in a large bun. Meredith genuinely loved people and made everyone feel at ease.

"Good morning, Meredith," Lauren said cheerfully.

Meredith put down the coffee mug she'd just taken a sip from. Her brown eyes twinkled. "Hello there! How was your Christmas?"

Lauren smiled. She was searching for a suitable response because she hadn't discussed her divorce with Meredith. So saying she'd holed up in a cabin while she wallowed in self-pity then had rescued a gorgeous hunk whom she had spent two days making love to, wouldn't do at all. She kept it simple and told a little white lie. "Wonderful. We went to the mountains. There was snow."

"I heard," said Meredith, "A blizzard. But I'm sure your mister kept you warm."

Lauren had found over the years that Meredith believed a little romance could cure anything that ailed you. Reading romance novels, which she could be found doing each day at lunchtime, was her favorite pastime.

"Oh, yes, I had a big strong man to keep me warm," Lauren confirmed. She smiled. It was the truth and it ought to satisfy Meredith's romantic imagination.

"And how was your Christmas?" she inquired.

"Too much family," Meredith complained. "The house was so full you were stepping over warm bodies to get to the bathroom. But we had a real good time."

"I'm glad to hear it." Lauren continued walking toward her office. "Have a great day!"

"You, too," Meredith said and resumed drinking her coffee.

At around ten that morning, Albert Lawrence tapped on her office door. Lauren could see his portly outline through the opaque glass in the top of the door.

"Come in, Albert," she called, her tone welcoming.

In his sixties, Albert had a head full of curly white hair, which he kept shorn close to his head. In spite of his excess weight, he was invariably impeccably dressed. Today he wore a dark blue pinstriped suit with a white dress shirt and a red silk tie. His dress shoes were always shined to a high gloss.

He closed the door behind him and approached Lauren's desk at a turtle's pace. "Hello, Lauren. I thought I'd drop by and see how you were doing. Holding up? I went through a stressful divorce myself some years ago. Initially, I didn't think I'd survive without her. She left me for a younger man, you know, and back then, the courts were always on the side of the mother when it came to custody rights. I not only stood to lose a wife, but my children. So, I understand what you're going through."

Lauren smiled. "Albert, I believe those are the most words you've ever strung together in a conversation with me."

She gestured to the chair in front of her desk. "Please, sit."

Albert looked at the chair as though he were debating whether to sit or not. Then, he sat down. "Only for a few minutes," he said, "I don't want to disturb your work flow."

"You're not," she assured him. Albert was a worrier. He was a talented architect who was not stingy with his knowledge. She'd learned so much from him over the years. "And I'm doing fine, really. I haven't given Adam much thought at all during my break."

"Good, good." Albert hedged.

But instantly Lauren knew something was wrong and it concerned her ex-husband. "You sound like you have something to tell me," Lauren said suspiciously.

Albert didn't like giving people bad news, and usually left that task, particularly when the need arose to fire someone, to one of the other senior partners. Albert simply didn't have it in him.

He looked at her, his dark brown eyes full of sympathy. "I wouldn't even mention this but you are the principal architect on the project. The client says your ex's company has put in a bid to build the hospital."

Lauren's expression didn't change. She had known that she would one day have to work with Adam's company. He owned one of the largest construction companies in the state. Architects had to go on sites and check to make sure the building was being constructed according to specifications. That didn't mean she would encounter Adam on her frequent visits to the site. In fact, as head of the company he probably delegated much of the onsite work to someone below him on the totem pole.

"Don't worry," she said to Albert. "Even if his company wins the bidding war, more than likely I'll never run into him."

Albert looked appeased as he rose. "I hope not," he said. "The way he treated you was atrocious. I don't want him to upset you further. Well, I should let you get back to work."

Lauren rose and walked him to the door. "Thanks for your concern, Albert. You're very nice to think of me."

Albert blushed and hurried out. Lauren closed the door and returned to her desk. *Somewhere in the city,* she thought, *that bastard is probably having a good laugh thinking that I'm trembling in my boots, dreading the possibility of having to interact with him. We'll see who gets the last laugh.*

She returned to her computer and the 3-D image she was working on. Architects used to spend hours building models of the structures they designed. The models were then presented to the client so that they could visualize how the finished project would look. More and more these days, models were built using computer programs and her presentation to the client was usually in the form of a PowerPoint slide show.

Her cell phone rang, and she picked it up and checked the display. It was her sister, Meghan. "What's up, Meg?"

"Are you free for lunch?"

"I was planning to work through lunch," she said regrettably. "Why?"

"You have an event to go to in less than forty-eight hours," Meghan reminded her. "Don't you think you should devote some time to shopping for it? Mina, Desi and I aren't going to let you wear something you've already worn before. Our reputations are at stake."

"What do you mean your reputations?" Lauren asked, amused.

"How you look reflects on us," Meghan said reasonably. "After all, you're the oldest and you're supposed to set the example. Although, God knows, you've never taken that seriously. But things have changed. You're divorced. Undoubtedly your ex is going to be at the ball with his barely legal fiancée and we're not going to let you go unless you're put together."

Lauren laughed. "Oh, I don't think he wants to go to jail. She's probably over eighteen."

Meghan snorted. "Yeah, he's such a prince."

Getting them back on subject, Lauren asked, "What are you going to do if I refuse to go shopping with you? Kidnap me?"

"If we have to," Mina cut in. "I can bench press two hundred pounds. I should be able to hogtie you."

"Fine," said Lauren, still laughing. "Pick me up out front at noon. Don't be late because I can only spare an hour for this shopping expedition of yours."

The girls were in Meghan's baby-blue Mustang when they pulled up to the curb. Desiree was riding shotgun so Lauren climbed in back with Amina. All of them were dressed differently. Meghan, with her long black wavy hair in a smooth chignon, was in a business suit like Lauren because she was taking off from work, too. Amina, who wore her black hair in a huge Afro, was the most casual of them all and was wearing jeans, athletic shoes and a leather jacket over a pullover shirt. She was not employed yet following her last hitch in the army. Desiree, who'd recently had her long hair shortened to chin length, was wearing a designer dress and shoes. She was the fashionista in the family and one who knew where to find designer clothes at bargain prices.

The air in the car was redolent with fast-food smells. "Where's my lunch?" Lauren asked, inhaling the enticing odor.

Desiree turned around and handed her a Wendy's bag and a large drink. "A single and a Diet Coke," she said.

"You remembered. Thank you," Lauren said, accepting the bag and paper cup. She sat back and ate in silence while her sisters debated where to go.

After deliberating, they headed to a consignment boutique downtown where Desiree knew the owner and he promised they would get their money's worth.

"You mean my money," Lauren said. "Remember, I don't have Adam's credit cards anymore. I'm on a single girl's budget."

"Don't worry," said Desiree. "We've decided to treat you."

"Yeah," put in Mina. "I've got a chunk of money in my account and no one to spend it on."

"Spend it on you," Lauren suggested. "You deserve to be spoiled with all you've been through."

Lauren immediately felt the mood change after she spoke and quickly regretted her words. Amina was a helicopter pilot and her last assignment had been in Afghanistan. She had been credited with saving hundreds of soldiers by air-lifting them to safety. Like many soldiers, she lived with the knowledge that each day she woke up in the morning could be her last day on earth. She was ready to lay down her life for her country. But when the man she loved was killed in action, she'd lost it. Six years in service seemed long enough. When Keith was alive she had thought she would make the military her life's calling. After all, he had been in it for life. But when he died, her heart was no longer in it. She didn't reenlist when her time ran its course.

Amina laughed shortly. "Stop tiptoeing around me, you guys! I'm handling it. And don't think I don't know what you've been thinking but have been afraid to say out loud. It's the Gaines girls' curse. First Desiree lost the man she loved and now I've lost the man I love." She met Lauren's gaze. "I'm sure you and Meg are wondering if the same thing's going to happen to you."

"Never," Lauren vehemently denied. "I don't think that way. My heart just goes out to you and Desi. I wish I could take the pain away."

"Well, I have," Meghan admitted softly. "I tried not to think that way but it makes you wonder. I mean, what are the odds that two sisters would lose the men they love, and both before marriage?"

"If you're going to think superstitiously," Lauren reasoned, "then Adam should have died before I married him. Instead, we were married for nearly six years, and he's still very much alive. There is no curse, just life, and life can be hard enough without adding a curse to the equation."

"Amen," agreed Desiree. "Let's leave the curse alone, shall we? There is nothing preventing us from being happy in a relationship except finding the right man and having moderate good fortune. After all, Momma and Daddy have been together for thirty-two years."

A few minutes later they were pulling up to the consignment shop. Once inside Lauren immediately began to model dresses while her sisters commented on her choices. Since women who attended the ball were asked to wear either a black dress or a white dress, Lauren selected dresses with only those colors. But after half an hour and no sure winner, Desiree handed her a vintage halter gown by Halston that was vertically half black and half white. Lauren tried it on and stood in front of the full-length mirror. It fit perfectly. The sisters gathered around her, approval written all over their faces.

The dress had an invisible zipper up the back and the material was thick and soft. It felt like silk against her skin. "I look like one of those 1930s pinup girls," she said wistfully.

"Wear your hair up," Desiree advised. "We want Colton to be able to see your bare back."

"And wear red lipstick to complete the 1930s pinup girl look," Amina chimed in.

"Of course, you might not even make it to the ball once Colton sees you in it," Meghan joked.

They all laughed.

Lauren smiled at her reflection. She couldn't wait.

The night of the ball, Colton got home late from work. Earlier that day he'd filled in for a welder on the downtown skyscraper site because the hired one hadn't shown up for work. Further investigation revealed he'd been in an accident. With no time to get anyone else, and with work in need of completion in a timely manner, Colton had gone on-site. Though, it wasn't unusual for him to get his hands dirty on the job. He'd started at the bottom. His dad had him working as a carpenter's helper when he was sixteen. By the time he was eighteen he was proficient at any number of skills from bricklaying to welding, plumbing and electrical wiring. His father told him he wanted to be able to say his son knew the business inside and out, and in the future when he became the head of the company it could be said that he'd earned the position.

As he entered his house, he was beginning to feel the effects of a long, physically taxing day. Then, he thought of Lauren and how she would look in her ball gown and he got a boost of energy. He hadn't seen her since the day of his dad's funeral. They had spoken several times, but both of them had been busy with work. He could see now that he was involved with a woman who enjoyed her work as much as he enjoyed his. He liked that about Lauren because he wanted her to be fulfilled. He was smart enough to know if a woman was happy with herself, she was more prone to be happy with her man.

He smiled as he showered. Was it too soon to think of himself as her man? Maybe, but he didn't care. He was going with the flow, eager to see where this would lead.

Thinking ahead, he'd laid out his clothing for the ball before he'd left for work that morning. The tuxedo was his. He'd stopped renting tuxes after thirty, believing a grown man, especially one who had occasion to wear a tux several times a year, should own at least one. It had been tailor-made to fit his wide shoulders, muscular chest, trim waist and long legs.

He switched out the cummerbund from time to time. He owned three different colors. Tonight he was simply wearing classic black. Lauren had told him her dress was black-and-white. He thought the traditional tux would complement her dress nicely.

He drove his Lexus to her house. The SUV was too sporty for tonight. When he rang the bell he felt a nervous tremor in his stomach. He tugged at his bow tie. He couldn't believe that after making love to her in every conceivable position up at the cabin he was anxious about taking her to a dance.

Lauren opened the door and flashed him a smile. "Wow, you really clean up well, Mr. Riley."

Colton was speechless. Her skin, her hair, the way her dress hugged her curves and, God help him, her juicy lips, all worked together. Her sexuality was personified even though the dress was not in the least immodest. No cleavage was spilling out of it. Her legs were entirely covered. Just her shoulders and back were bare and that was enough. Her golden-brown skin with its red undertones glowed with health. Her hair shone. Her eyes were clear and beautiful.

"If you don't say something soon I'm going to think you don't like my dress," Lauren teased.

Colton snapped out of his reverie and pulled her in his arms and kissed her. Lauren smiled at him when they parted. "That's more like it."

"You're exquisite," he said huskily. He held her face in his hands. "Maybe we can skip the ball."

Lauren laughed. "No, we're not skipping the ball. I'd have to tell Meghan she was right."

"What?" Colton asked.

"I'll explain on the way," she promised and grabbed her clutch and wrap from the foyer table.

The grand ballroom at the Marriott was more than five thousand square feet and elegantly furnished. Large round tables were placed around the periphery on the room. The chairs around the tables were uphol-stered with gold brocade fabric. Navy blue tablecloths topped the tables and elaborately folded gold cloth napkins adorned the white china. Centerpieces con-sisting of deep red long-stemmed roses in clear glass vases claimed pride of place at each table.

Two-hundred and fifty couples were in attendance. Colton and Lauren immediately spotted the Riley table and made their way across the ballroom past the highly polished wood dance floor and the podium.

"You made it just in time," Veronica greeted them. "They're getting ready to start serving."

She rose and accepted Colton's peck on the cheek. Then she and Lauren exchanged a greeting. Also at the table were Jade and Manu, Veronica's escort and nephew, Decker, and three other couples associated with Riley Construction.

"Lauren, you look lovely this evening," Veronica said with warmth.

"And you, Veronica," Lauren returned. "Your dress is stunning."

Veronica wore a simple sleeveless V-neck black gown. With her gold highlights and gold jewelry, she was the epitome of style and sophistication.

"Thank you," Veronica said. "Jade picked it out."

"Good call, Jade," Lauren complimented her. "You look fabulous tonight also. That gold brings out your eyes."

Jade had on a white gown with gold accents including a thick gold belt at her waist.

"You can't go wrong with classic lines," Jade said, smiling gratefully.

"What about us? Aren't we pretty?" Manu said, gesturing to himself and then Decker.

Manu and Decker were attired in black tuxedos similar to Colton's.

Jade laughed. "*Pretty* is not a word I would use to describe you, Manu. *Imposing* would be a better description. Shoulders like yours do not belong in a tuxedo. But Decker's kind of pretty tonight."

Decker frowned at his cousin. "Don't start with me,

cuz. People are already going to wonder if I can get a date on my own since I'm here with Auntie."

Veronica looked affronted. "Nobody twisted your arm. You wanted to come. I'm sorry Desiree wouldn't come with you but you don't have to take your disappointment out on us."

Decker appealed to Lauren. "What's wrong with your sister? Why won't she go out with me?"

"There's the problem right there," Veronica pointed out. "You asked what's wrong with Desiree. You should have asked what's wrong with you."

"There's nothing wrong with me," Decker proclaimed. "I'm one of the most eligible bachelors in Raleigh. I have a great job, I'm good-looking, healthy and I've got money in the bank. What else does she want in a man?"

"I can't speak for Desi," Lauren said. "I don't know why she won't go out with you. You'll have to ask her."

"Yes," said Veronica. "Go to the source."

Decker rose. "I will." He took his cell phone from the inside pocket of his jacket. "Excuse me."

In his absence, Veronica said, "That boy has it bad." She whispered to Lauren, "You can tell me, I won't say a word. Why won't she go out with him?"

Before Lauren could answer, Colton interjected hoping to change the subject. "Don't worry about Decker. He always lands on his feet."

The event's host, a distinguished-looking silver-haired man in a black tuxedo, walked onto the stage and spoke into the microphone at the podium. "Good evening, ladies and gentlemen, and welcome to the fiftieth annual Black and White Ball."

Shortly after the host finished speaking, a small army of waitstaff began serving dinner, which was a choice between prime rib, lobster or vegetarian lasagna with various side dishes. Decker returned after everyone had been served. He sat down and began to eat.

Veronica looked at him and asked, "Well, what did she say?"

"She said she won't go out with me because I'm not ready for her yet. She says I may never be ready for her." He sighed. "I have no idea what that means."

Veronica shook her head sadly. "No, I don't believe you do."

While they ate their meals, Lauren looked around the room. She recognized several couples at nearby tables, including a woman who had been in the ladies' room last year when Adam's mistress had confronted her. The woman was African American and looked to be in her forties. She was tall and shapely and wore her natural hair in a very short Afro. She caught Lauren watching her and smiled.

Lauren smiled back. She hoped seeing the woman would be the only thing to happen tonight to remind her of last year's embarrassment. But walking toward their table was Adam Eckhart, with a voluptuous woman in white on his arm.

Lauren hadn't seen him in months. She couldn't discern anything different about his six-foot frame. He was still fit. His goatee was expertly trimmed.

Grooming and presentation meant a great deal to him. He looked perfect in his black tux.

He stopped beside her chair. Lauren steeled herself for an insult of some kind.

"Good evening, Lauren," he said pleasantly. She hadn't realized it until now that when she'd spotted him she'd put her hand on Colton's thigh to steady herself. Now she felt his thigh muscles tighten reflexively. He clearly was not glad to see Adam, either.

She squeezed his thigh underneath the table, communicating to him to calm down. She could handle this. "Good evening, Adam," she said as she looked up at him.

"Riley," Adam directed at Colton with a slight smirk across his face.

"Eckhart," Colton replied. The two men's eyes met. Neither of their expressions was friendly.

"This is my fiancée, Nichole Kelly," Adam said, smiling at her.

Nichole was in her early twenties. Tall and buxom, her gown displayed her full breasts for all to see and admire. Lauren thought spillage was imminent. Knowing Adam, however, Lauren could not be certain that she'd chosen her own gown. Adam was very controlling. He'd probably told her what to wear, what to say and how to say it.

"Miss Kelly," Lauren said politely.

"I love your gown," Nichole Kelly replied a bit breathlessly.

"Thank you," Lauren said, a bit stunned. She seemed sweet.

Adam, looking irritated by Nichole's behavior, went

on, "Did you hear I won the bid on the children's hospital?"

"No, I left work early today and haven't listened to my messages," Lauren said stiffly. She was not going to congratulate him. His coming over here was a ploy to unnerve her and possibly get a dig in at Colton.

Colton congratulated him, though. "Good for you, Eckhart."

Adam smiled. "Thank you. I noticed your company didn't have a bid in."

"No, we already have enough to keep us busy for a while," Colton was pleased to note.

"Excellent," said Adam. His gaze rested on Lauren. "This will give me the opportunity work with Lauren. When we were married we never got to work together. It'll be a new experience for me, and I like challenges. Good evening, all." With that he turned and led his fiancée away.

"What a pompous ass," Veronica said after he was out of earshot. "Lauren, are you okay?"

"I'm fine," Lauren assured her, but she was fuming inside.

Chapter 8

"That man is so irritating," Lauren said for Colton's ears only. "He only came over here to plant seeds of discontent in us. He can't stand to see me happy. And what's up with Nichole Kelly? She seems almost sweet. As if she's unaware of what kind of man she's with."

Colton's gaze locked with hers. "Mission accomplished, then, huh? Here you are carrying on about him. Are you going to let him spoil our evening?"

Lauren rolled her eyes. "As if you didn't want to punch his lights out," she accused. "I could feel how tense you were."

He didn't try to deny it. "I've made no secret of the fact I can't stand him. But I wouldn't have hit him."

In the background the band started to play and the

host again took the stage. "I hope everyone's enjoying their meals. Now it's time to get up and dance the night away. Let's bring in 2014 on a high note!"

"Good idea," said Colton, reaching for Lauren's hand. "Let's dance."

Lauren was glad to get up and stretch her legs. They were among the first couples to walk onto the dance floor. Above them a crystal chandelier sparkled with golden light. The band's chanteuse, a lovely young African American woman in a black gown, began singing Alicia Keys's latest hit.

She sang it with soulful intensity. The speed with which she sang was just right for slow-dancing. Lauren relaxed in Colton's arms and gazed up at him. He smiled tenderly. She regretted bringing Adam up. She had vowed she wouldn't allow his little games to get to her. Now here she was, tense, because of something he'd said. He couldn't have been serious about looking forward to working with her on the children's hospital.

"I'm sorry," she said sincerely.

"Baby, I'm holding you in my arms," Colton said softly. "No apology needed."

She sighed and laid her head on his chest. The thump of his steady heartbeat steadied her. Closing her eyes she let him lead her, her trust in him implicit. She could feel the powerful muscles in his thigh where his leg touched hers. As she relaxed she was becoming aroused. The song was so sexy. Images of them making love came unbidden to her mind's eye.

Colton tried to control his emotions. He wanted to be aware of everything about Lauren in this moment. But when he did that he was also aware of the warmth of her body, the soft seductiveness of her skin, her scent and the rhythm of her heart. Because he was unable to separate his desire for her from her physical being he was soon turned on by her closeness. Plus there was the fact that he'd been dreaming of making love to her ever since he'd left her on Christmas Day a week ago. It had been a whole week since they'd been intimate, which was too long.

Lauren looked into his eyes. He knew she could feel his erection.

"Do you want to get out of here?" she asked playfully. "Find an empty closet somewhere?"

He chuckled at her suggestion. "I'm shocked you would say such a thing, Miss Gaines. Give me a minute. I'll calm down."

"You've got that kind of control?" she asked innocently. "Maybe you can teach me how to do that."

"You, too?" he asked, his eyes smoldering.

She loved those smoky-gray eyes of his. She'd heard of women being seduced by a pair of sexy eyes but it had never happened to her until she'd met him.

"Yes," she happily confessed. "I've been unable to stop imagining you naked and on top of me for any length of time since we parted." She peered deeply into his eyes. "And in my nighttime dreams I'm insatiable. The problem is I know the reality is as good, or better, than my dreams. So you see I'm a lost cause. Because of you I'm completely obsessed with sex. I was a normal person until you showed up."

"I'm sorry?" Colton said with a beguiling smile.

"You should be," she teased.

"I'm sure you'll think of ways to punish me later," Colton said, not looking apologetic in the least. And his erection was not going away as he'd promised.

"Why wait for later?" Lauren asked. "I'm going to punish you now." She wrapped her arms around his neck and drew him down for a long, sensual kiss. Her tongue sweetly caressed his and the sensation was orgasmic.

When they came up for air, he grinned at her. "You're a bad girl."

She smiled. "So, punish me!"

But Colton was aware that they had become the center of attention and refrained from meeting her challenge there on the dance floor. He pulled her back in position and they resumed dancing. "Behave yourself. We're becoming a spectacle."

At his company's table, Adam watched them with fascination. He had come here tonight relatively certain that Lauren would be in attendance. However, he was shocked to see her on Colton Riley's arm. He knew he was being unreasonable but the fact that she was involved with his biggest business rival felt like a personal affront. Of all the men in Raleigh, or the world for that matter, she was with him?

"Sweetie, let's dance," Nichole pleaded.

He smiled indulgently at her and rose, offering her his hand.

She giggled. He hated it when she giggled. She sounded even younger than her twenty-two years. Intellectually, she was nowhere near being his match. But she was stunning and very susceptible to suggestion. Already she was willing to do anything to please him. Of course, her malleability got tiresome after a while. Once you had someone under your thumb it was inevitable that you would lose respect for that person.

As he held Nichole in his arms his attention was riveted on Lauren and Riley as they danced a few feet away. There hadn't been another kiss after that outrageous public display they'd put on. Lauren was becoming a cliché, a divorced woman who played fast and loose with her reputation, he thought.

Colton and Lauren returned to their table and Colton asked his mother to dance.

"No, I'm fine," Veronica graciously declined. "I'm fine just watching you all."

"Mom, when you and Dad attended this affair you were always on the dance floor. Let's go." Colton would not take no for an answer.

Veronica took her son's arm. "Very well," she said resignedly. "If only to prevent your father from visiting me in my dreams and accusing me of moping without him."

After they'd gone, Jade said to Lauren, "She's not joking. Since Dad's death she's dreamed about him every night. I'm beginning to think she lives for her dreams about him. I'm trying not to worry."

Lauren had some experience in this area. "There's nothing wrong with Veronica. People who're widowed often dream about their spouses. It helps with the grieving process. My Grandpa Beck dreamed about my grandmother a lot after she died but the dreams have tapered off. Now he only dreams about her every once in a while. That doesn't mean he loves her less. It's just that he's accepted she's gone and his mind's at peace. At least that's how he explained it."

Jade smiled at her. "Thanks for that, Lauren. You put my mind at ease."

"She's a worrywart," Manu said. "Always has been."

"Come on and dance with me," Jade told him, pulling him up by the hand. "Work off some of that prime rib."

Lauren sat watching them once they were on the dance floor. Manu moved surprisingly well for a big man. Jade's dance skills were obviously more advanced than his but from the brilliant smile on her face, Lauren could tell she was having a wonderful time in her husband's arms.

After a couple of songs, a male singer replaced the chanteuse. His song was one designed for lovers. Lauren spotted Colton and Veronica leaving the dance floor.

When they got back to the table, Veronica was laughing. "I don't think I'll ever get used to songs that openly talk about sex," she said. "In my day it was inferred but not explicitly so." She smiled at Lauren. "He's all yours, dear."

Colton laughed as he held out his hand to Lauren, "Sweetheart?"

Lauren smiled when he referred to her as *sweet-*

heart. Up until now, only *baby* had been his term of endearment for her.

Colton planted a kiss on the side of her neck as she settled in his arms. "Mom was right. This is not the type of song you dance with your mother to. This is baby-making music."

"Then I'd better sit this one out, too."

Colton laughed again. "Do you know how much fun you are to be with? Your beauty and accomplishments aside, you're still one of the most fascinating women I've ever known. But I had a clue you would be when you opened the door with a gun in your hand."

"We were in the middle of nowhere," she reminded him. "You could have been the Abominable Snowman for all I knew."

"I never asked, but do you have a permit to carry a gun?"

"Yes, Officer," she quipped. "Plus, I've put in many hours at the shooting gallery. The general made sure of that. We practiced shooting like other kids practiced their basketball game. It was just another pastime that we enjoyed and were proficient at."

"What else did the general make sure you girls were trained to do?"

"Hand-to-hand combat was taught and we were put in a martial arts class when we turned seven," Lauren said. "For physical conditioning, not to learn to kick someone's butt. Our sensei stressed respect and control of anger. We were taught that martial arts were only to be used in self-defense or to protect someone else."

"Which discipline?" Colton asked.

"A lot of kids were in tae kwon do," Lauren said, "But the general signed us up for karate. He said it was more suited to a woman's body."

"Why is that?"

"Karate is the Japanese art of self-defense in which blows and kicks are targeted to sensitive parts of the opponent's body. Women have more strength in their lower bodies, so the general believed women would be very adept at kicking the crap out of anyone who attacked them."

"And were you good at it?" asked Colton, his eyes alight with humor.

"I earned a black belt by the time I was seventeen," Lauren said without a trace of bragging.

Colton laughed softly. "I'm impressed." He hugged her tightly and wistfully said, "Why didn't mom and dad invite you to the house years ago when you were neighbors in the mountains? We've got a lot of time to make up."

Lauren was touched. "Your parents did invite me to their home here in Raleigh, but I politely declined. Adam tolerated my associating with them in the mountains because the cabin's isolated. But here in Raleigh it would have gotten out that I was a friend of the Rileys. In his mind you all are the enemy."

Colton sighed. "You're right. It's all in his mind because I rarely give him a thought let alone think of him as my rival. He's the one who started this by bribing people to beat us out of at least two contracts that I know of. Personally, I wish he'd realize that there's enough work to go around without resorting to such tactics."

"There's a possibility he has a screw loose," Lauren offered with a laugh. "And I'm not saying that because I'm bitter. Okay, maybe I'm a little bitter. There's nothing wrong with a woman being a little bitter. It's my prerogative to be bitter. Long live the bitter!"

Colton laughed. "You crack me up."

She laughed, too. "Okay, I'm not leaving the house without my meds anymore."

Colton kissed her forehead. "You're even more beautiful when you let go and laugh like that."

Following their dance Colton escorted her back to their table, after which he went to the men's room. When he was returning from the facilities he encountered Adam coming in the opposite direction in the corridor.

He had planned to simply ignore him, but Adam was having none of that. "You know, Riley," he said, "I thought taking my sloppy seconds when it comes to business would be enough for you. But no, you had to try out my ex-wife, as well. That's poor sportsmanship."

Instantly angered by his vulgar suggestion, Colton stopped short and stared at Adam. His big hands balled into fists of rage. His gray eyes became even more stormy than usual as they narrowed and focused on

Adam. "You are one small-minded prick, Eckhart, if you think that Lauren is a possession that you once owned. What happened? You realized you've made a mistake by letting her go? Sloppy seconds, you say? Lauren is nobody's sloppy seconds. She's wonderful and you know it. That's why it rankles that she's finding happiness after being shackled to you for years." He circled Adam and their actions were beginning to draw the attention of passersby who stopped to observe them.

"Happiness," Adam scoffed. He chuckled. "You believe you can make her happy? Did you even go to college? You're a roughneck. You still do menial jobs. Oh, yes, I heard about that. You probably think it makes you a part of the team. But real powerbrokers know that you have to separate yourself from the team. You have to stand above them. Your father's death was the worst thing that could have happened to Riley Construction. Your leadership will bankrupt it within the year. You're a boy trying to fill your old man's shoes."

"I'm not going to stand here and defend myself against accusations that are unfounded," Colton said. "Time will tell whether or not I'm fit to run my family's company. Time will also tell whether or not I can make Lauren happy. But there's one thing we both already know. She's not with you, she's with me. And that's where she wants to be."

"I could get her back if I wanted to," Adam calmly claimed with a smirk. "She was in love with me once.

I can get her to fall in love with me again. Care to make a wager?"

"There's nothing you won't stoop to, is there?" Colton wondered aloud, genuinely taken aback by his crassness.

"Are you afraid you're going to lose?" Adam sneered. "Because, my friend, you don't stand a chance since for the next year or so I'm going to be spending a lot of time with Lauren on the children's hospital project. I'll probably see her more than you. Lauren and I have a past. I assure you she still has feelings for me. You don't just stop loving someone because you're no longer together."

"What about your fiancée?" Colton asked.

"She's a dalliance, a pretty distraction," Adam said nonchalantly.

"You really do have a screw loose," Colton told him, shaking his head in wonder.

Adam was outraged. Colton's words suggested that he'd been discussing his sanity with someone, and that someone could only have been Lauren. "Is that what she said about me?" he yelled. "That I have a screw loose?"

Colton was silent on the matter. He gestured to the audience they'd attracted. "You're making a case for that right now."

Several of the men and women who'd gathered around them nodded in agreement.

"Can we have some privacy?" Adam yelled at them.

"This is a public hallway, bruh," said one of the

men. He was also dressed in a tuxedo. "I've got your back, Colton, if something jumps off."

Colton acknowledged the guy's offer with a nod in his direction. "Thanks, Joe, but nothing's going to jump off. The theatrics are over." He glanced at his watch as he turned to leave. "It's nearly midnight. I'm going to usher in the New Year with my lady."

"Remember what I said," Adam called after him. "She'll be mine again within the year."

"Keep dreaming," Colton said in parting.

Adam stood alone, fuming. A screw loose, indeed. He would show them exactly how it felt to go up against someone who was as determined to succeed at whatever they set their mind on as he was. Lauren had been the one to begin divorce proceedings. He had asked her, begged her—and he was not the sort of man to beg—to forgive his infidelity and continue their marriage. But she said that she had lived for a long time with the suspicion that he was cheating on her and now that she had proof she could not go on fooling herself. It was over. From that point on, what could he do but put on an act and tell her that she'd never supported him anyway? If she had been the wife he needed her to be he wouldn't have sought solace elsewhere. That had torn her up. He still remembered the hurtful expression in her eyes. He couldn't back down then though. He told her a man of his standing deserved a trophy wife. She was getting a little long in the tooth.

He'd in essence bitten off his nose to spite his face.

He'd made a mistake. Now that he was engaged to the trophy-wife-to-be, he'd tried to be satisfied. But Riley was right. He did want Lauren back. That old saying, you don't miss the water until the well runs dry, was true.

The baiting of Riley was simply a way to strengthen his resolve to win Lauren back. He was fired up now. He'd prove to Riley that he wasn't a man to be counted out.

Chapter 9

Colton tried to shake off the madness that had ensued in the hallway as he strode back into the ballroom. His eyes went directly to his table where his mother and Lauren seemed to be deep in conversation. They were leaning toward one another, their heads nearly touching. The warm feeling he got from knowing how much his mother and Lauren enjoyed each other's company almost dispelled the seed of doubt his confrontation with Adam Eckhart had planted in him.

Could Lauren still have feelings for Eckhart? He was at war with his conscience. On one hand he wanted to be completely honest with Lauren and tell her exactly what had transpired a few minutes ago. On the other, he didn't want to ruin her evening by telling her about Eckhart's lunacy. So he decided he'd tell her later.

His mother smiled up at him when he joined them. "Colton, did you know that both Lauren's mother and I attended Shaw University? Now, I've got to go look in my old yearbooks and see if I can find a Virginia Beck. Beck's her maiden name."

Sitting down on Lauren's left Colton said, "No, I didn't. You two might have known one another."

Veronica frowned. "Seems like I would remember a Virginia, but I don't."

Lauren smiled at Colton. She looked into his eyes and seemed, to him, to detect that something was amiss. Or maybe it was his guilt at deciding not to tell her about his encounter with Eckhart until later that was niggling at him.

A look of askance crossed her face. "Is something wrong?" she said, her tone soft but urgent.

Ever since Lauren had seen Adam again she'd had this sense of foreboding lying just below the surface, trying its best to rear its ugly head.

"No, no," Colton assured her and rubbed her arm comfortingly. He leaned toward her, kissed her cheek and whispered, "It's almost midnight."

Around them, couples were returning to their tables from the dance floor. Tradition at the Black and White Ball dictated that at the stroke of midnight, champagne would flow like water and everyone would toast the New Year in.

Waitstaff entered the ballroom pushing trolleys laden with bottles of the bubbly spirits. On stage the host was counting down the seconds. "Ten, nine, eight, seven," he intoned.

Promptly at the midnight hour the sound of corks popping filled the ballroom. "Happy New Year!" everyone exclaimed with joy. Those who had them blew paper horns. Silver and gold confetti rained on them.

At Colton and Lauren's table, champagne glasses were filled and everyone offered toasts to one another. Colton looked into Lauren's eyes and said, his voice husky, "I hope this year will be the best you've ever had."

"It will be with you in it," Lauren said, smiling happily.

They gently touched their glasses together, took sips of champagne and put their glasses on the table.

Colton leaned in, his gaze on her mouth. "Our first kiss of the year," he said, his voice rife with longing.

"Make it a good one," she whispered back as she wrapped her arms around his neck and pulled him down to meet her mouth.

They got lost in one another. The rest of the world receded as if there was only the two of them, high on the euphoria that new love causes. When they parted and peered into each other's eyes both of them knew something vital had changed between them.

"Colton," Veronica said.

To Colton her voice sounded far away. Then, he came back to the present and realized that hadn't been the first time she'd tried to get his attention.

He smiled at his mother. "I'm sorry. What did you say?"

"I was saying," Veronica said with a laugh, "that I'm going home." She rose and the rest of the family got to their feet also. Everyone had varying amounts of confetti in their hair and on their clothing and was picking it off themselves. "I hate this stuff," Veronica complained.

She looked around for her nephew, but Decker was nowhere in sight. She sighed. "When Decker gets back," she said to Colton and Lauren, "tell him as an escort, he sucks."

Then she hugged Lauren and Colton. "Enjoy the rest of your evening."

She left with Jade and Manu, with Manu giving Colton a thumbs-up on the way out.

Colton and Lauren were left at the table alone. The other Riley Construction staff and their dates were on the dance floor. For many, the party really got started after midnight.

Lauren smiled at Colton. "Going home sounds good to me."

Colton was about to say something when her cell phone started making its distinct text message buzzing sound that reminded her of a tiny chainsaw. She laughed thinking it was probably one of her sisters texting to say Happy New Year.

"Excuse me," she said to Colton as she slipped her hand into her clutch and got her cell phone. Quickly pressing a couple buttons she frowned and murmured, "Oh, no, no, it can't be."

When tears sprang to her eyes and she thrust the cell phone at Colton as if she wanted it far away from her, Colton's first impulse was to comfort her. He pulled her into his arms and held her against his chest as he read what was on the cell phone's screen. The message consisted of only four words. *I still love you.* And it was from Adam Eckhart.

"Please erase it," Lauren said as she clung to him.

Colton did as she asked. Then pressed the phone back into her hand. "It's gone, sweetheart." He pulled her to her feet. "Come on. Let's go home."

Lauren wiped the tears away with the pad of her thumb as they made their way across the ballroom to the exit. "Why doesn't he just leave me alone?" she wondered aloud as Colton made sure her wrap was securely around her before they ventured out into the chilly night.

"Sweetheart, we need to talk," he said, "but not here. Let's wait until we're in the car on the way to your place."

She nodded numbly, sniffing. "I hate him so much," she said, her voice barely a whisper.

Colton was in a pensive mood for the first few minutes as they drove along the streets of downtown Raleigh. Traffic was light at the moment since most revelers were already where they wanted to be.

Why had Lauren reacted with tears when she'd gotten Eckhart's text message? Why not with derision, or laughter, calling him a nut or a sap to send such an idiotic admission of love to his ex-wife? There were many ways she could have reacted, but tears? Tears were connected to emotions. She apparently still felt something for him.

"Lauren, on my way back from the restroom I ran into Eckhart and against my better judgment I let him draw me into an argument."

Lauren turned in her seat so that she could see his face while he spoke. "What did you argue about?"

"You," Colton said, his voice cracking. He cleared his throat. "I don't want to go into detail because some things were said that were inflammatory, things I don't want to have to repeat. But the gist of it was he's angry with me for dating you and he threatened to do everything in his power to get you back."

Lauren gave a great sigh of relief. "So he threw down the gauntlet," she said with a short laugh, "challenged you to a duel at dawn and attempted to make a gentleman's bet on who would come out on top?"

Colton looked at her, amazed by her change of attitude. "What brought back the Lauren with backbone? A minute ago you were crying."

"That was before I knew that this was just another one of his games," she explained. "I got emotional when I got the text because I thought he was genuinely still in love with me and he was going to make an effort to get back in my life. That part terrified me, but it's not unheard of for a divorced couple to reconcile. Not that I had any intention of doing so. But I remember the love I used to have for him, too, and occasionally it tries to break through to the surface. Those are the times I suffer and wonder what I did wrong to make him cheat on me."

"A cheater is a cheater no matter the provocation,"

Colton said. "I sincerely believe that. You didn't do anything for him to cheat on you."

She smiled at him. "I know that now but for months after I had filed for divorce I wavered between righteous indignation and feeling that maybe I should take some blame for his actions, too. Anyway, I no longer believe I did anything for him to go looking for a mistress."

"So, why do you think he's playing games with you and he's not sincere about still being in love with you?"

"It's that old rivalry thing again," Lauren said calmly. "You have something he believes is rightfully his. *Me.* If he hadn't approached you tonight and said all those things you're avoiding telling me because you think my feelings will be hurt, I would have taken that text message seriously." She sighed again and ran her hand over his muscular thigh. "Let him try his best. There's only one man I'm interested in and I'm touching him right now. And as soon as I get him home I'm going to be touching him all over."

Colton let out a soft sigh of his own. The sound of her sexy voice and the feel of her hand on his thigh aroused him. He was glad he'd come straight to her and told her about his conversation with Eckhart. Now that their cards were on the table there was nothing left that could come between them. In a few minutes not even their clothes would be separating them. He would see to that as soon as they walked through the door of her apartment. He pressed down a little harder on the accelerator of the Lexus.

* * *

She had him flat on his back on the thick rug atop the hardwood floor of the living room. They hadn't made it to the bedroom before they'd begun ripping their clothes off. The lamps on the end tables were dimmed and the room was quiet except for their heavy breaths.

Their naked bodies in two shades of brown, his dark cinnamon, hers more caramel, were joined in a timeless dance. Lauren's head was thrown back in ecstasy, her full breasts shaking with each thrust. Colton gave her every inch of him. She reveled in it and her body asked for more.

Unable to keep her orgasm at bay any longer, Lauren's thrusts increased in frequency and the climax claimed her at the same moment as Colton came with a ferocity that made him want to howl. He controlled it and groaned loudly instead.

Lauren moaned languidly and lay on his chest, her vaginal walls quivering around his shaft with her release. She peered into his eyes, her own dreamy. A smile turned up the corners of her generous mouth. "Now, that's how Cinderella should end her night at the ball."

Colton smiled and hugged her tightly. "I'm glad you enjoyed yourself."

Two weeks later, Lauren attended the groundbreaking ceremony for the new children's hospital. It was a Monday morning and the January air was cold, the wind brisk and the sunshine bright.

Lauren sat on the platform that had been erected for the occasion, waiting to get up and say a few words after the director of the hospital introduced her as the architect. Local news stations were covering the event and there were perhaps two hundred people sitting on folding chairs in the cleared field that was the site for the hospital.

Adam sat on the opposite side of the podium at which the hospital's director was delivering his welcome speech. Lauren had made the mistake of making eye contact with Adam on one occasion but he'd looked so hopeful she had refused to look at him again. Since the night of the ball he had sent multiple text messages. None of which she'd responded to.

After the groundbreaking ceremony, the media briefly interviewed both Lauren and Adam. She finished first and beat a hasty retreat. He caught up with her on the street where she'd parked the Range Rover.

"Lauren, Lauren," he cried, running across the street, car horns blaring at him.

He was wearing a dark blue suit with a black overcoat. His goatee looked freshly trimmed. Lauren stood with her back to the driver's side door of the Range Rover, her eyes narrowed.

"I have nothing to say to you," she warned as he stopped in front of her and opened his mouth to speak.

Adam clamped his mouth shut and took a deep breath. Then he gave a hopeless shrug and started talking. "Well, I've got something to say to you. I'm forty years old and I'm still immature. Instead of appreciating you when we were together I did nothing but find fault with you, which is something I now realize I did because I was so in awe of you. There was nothing wrong with you. Instead, there was something wrong with my values. Money and position were the only things I cared about and I thought that you didn't fit into my plans. I accused you of not supporting me. It was I who didn't support you. I can see that now."

"Hold on a minute," Lauren told him as she opened her car door, leaned inside and ejected a CD from the CD player. She put the CD back in its case and handed it to Adam. "Listen to track four," she told him.

A few minutes later after he'd watched her drive away and walked back to his SUV Adam put the CD in his CD player and jumped to track four. "I don't believe a word you say…" Ben Harper sang.

Smiling, Adam relaxed on the car seat. He had to give it to her. She had style.

Lauren looked at Adam in her rearview mirror. She remembered when his charm didn't seem in the least bit smarmy to her. She'd eaten it up. She'd been thrilled that he was interested in her at all. When they'd met he was already a successful builder and because of his success and his attractiveness to women, he was considered one of the best catches in Raleigh. In spite of objections from her parents who after meeting him later told her in private that he was not to be trusted, she had given him her heart. Thinking of her parents reminded her that she was taking Colton to Sunday dinner at her parents' house this weekend. She wondered what they would say about him in private after meeting him.

* * *

"I'm nervous about meeting your dad," Colton admitted on the drive to Lauren's parents' home on the outskirts of Raleigh.

Lauren tried to laugh it off. "You're not the first guy who's been nervous about meeting the general. But I'm going to let you in on a secret—he's not the one to look out for. That would be Momma. Daddy's easygoing. All he cares about on a Sunday afternoon is the amount of time he gets in front of the TV watching football. He's devoted to North Carolina State and you follow that team, too, so you already have one thing in common. With Momma, no man is good enough for her daughters, period. Even if she likes you you're still not good enough. So, I suggest you relax and be yourself."

"And your sisters?" he asked.

"Don't worry about my sisters. They think you're perfect for me. They're very smart girls, my sisters."

When they pulled into the driveway, Virginia was standing in the doorway, a warm smile on her face. "Colton, it's a pleasure to meet you finally." She shook his hand and led him into the family room with Lauren bringing up the rear.

The large family room was furnished in comfortable leather seating. The décor was more suited to a man's tastes with dark brown being the dominant color. Colton was introduced to Lauren's father who got up and shook his hand. Fonzi was a couple inches taller than he was, but Colton had broader shoulders and he was more muscular. "Good to meet you, Colton," said Fonzi. "Let me introduce you to my father-in-law, Benjamin Beck."

Benjamin Beck was small and wiry with solid white wavy hair that he wore long and tied back with a strip of leather. His dark brown skin was weathered from the outdoors and his jeans and plaid shirt were a bit frayed but clean. He was a man without pretension, and Colton liked him instantly.

Benjamin firmly shook his hand. "I knew your father. He was a good man."

Colton smiled. "Thank you, sir. It's good to meet you. Lauren tells me you own a hunting lodge. I'd love to see it someday."

Benjamin laughed shortly. "Oh, there's not much to it. Just plain old logs, the bare bones, I'm afraid. The people who stay at the lodge are looking to get back to nature."

"Well, I like the outdoors," said Colton. "I'm not a hunter but I fish and enjoy outdoor sports."

"Then we ought to go fishing sometime," Benjamin said. He smiled at Lauren as if to say, "I like this one."

"Daddy, before you all start planning a fishing trip let me introduce Colton to the rest of the family," Lauren cut in sweetly.

Colton had already met Desiree since she had accompanied Lauren to his father's funeral and come with her to the house afterward. But he had yet to meet Meghan and Amina. He saw a resemblance to Lauren in each of them. Their eyes were almond-shaped like hers. They also had Lauren's honey-brown skin tone. They were all attractive women and apparently enjoyed exercising because they were physically fit and healthy-looking. Knowing what Lauren had told him about their father teaching them to shoot and signing them up for karate classes at the age of seven, he could see his influence on them.

"Hi again," Desiree said and came forward to offer a hug.

Colton hugged her back. "Desiree," he said warmly. "My cousin sends his best."

Desiree laughed. "You tell him I send mine right back."

Amina was next. She had her natural hair braided and it fell to the middle of her back. She shook his hand. "Amina," she said.

"Like the African warrior princess?" Colton said.

Amina was impressed. "You know about Aminatu, the Nigerian princess who built a fortress around the city of Zaria to protect her people in times of war?"

"I'm an African history buff," Colton admitted.

This earned him points from Virginia, who was an educator.

She continued with the introductions. "And this is the baby of the family, Meghan."

Meghan smiled up at him. "It's a pleasure, Colton. I happen to be a history professor."

Colton peered at her with a puzzled expression. "You can't be more than twenty."

"I'm twenty-four, the youngest professor at North Carolina State," she told him matter-of-factly. She laughed, "I don't really look twenty, do I?"

"I'm sorry, but you do," said Colton.

Everyone laughed.

"All right, since the introductions have been made," Virginia announced, "Colton, have a seat and enjoy the game. Girls, I know this is sexist, but let's get the food on the table."

Her daughters let out playful groans of protest as they followed her out of the room.

In the women's absence, Fonzi turned to Colton, who had sat down beside him on the big brown leather couch in front of the widescreen TV. "That's just an excuse to go talk about you behind your back."

"Oh, I know," said Colton. "That's how they do it in my family, too."

Fonzi chuckled and reached for the bowl of mixed nuts, but his father-in-law already had it in his hands and was picking out the pecans and putting them in his mouth.

"May I have the nuts, Ben?" asked Fonzi.

"You could stand to drop a few pounds," Ben teased him. "I'm doing you a favor."

"You'd be doing me a favor by passing me the nuts," Fonzi insisted.

"Wait, there's another pecan at the bottom," Benjamin said.

"Ginny!" Fonzi yelled. "Would you tell your father to behave?"

"Behave, Daddy," Virginia yelled back.

Benjamin handed over the bowl of nuts. "Big baby," he muttered about his son-in-law.

Fonzi peered into the bowl, which had been totally

depleted of his favorite nut, the pecan. "You don't even like pecans," he accused Benjamin.

"I suddenly get a taste for them when I'm around you," Ben said with a smile.

Fonzi sighed and shook his head. "One of these days, old man, one of these days."

"Let's go," said Benjamin as if he were ready to step outside. He said to Colton conspiratorially, "His bark is worse than his bite."

Fonzi set the bowl of nuts on the coffee table. "Let me explain, Colton. Benjamin has never forgiven me for marrying his daughter and making her happy. He thought she should have stayed in the mountains with him and married some mountain man and stayed barefoot and pregnant instead of getting an education and traveling the world with me. And that, in a nutshell, is the reason for the antagonism between me and my father-in-law, the most stubborn man in creation."

"That's not all," Benjamin said. "I also don't like you because you didn't give me a grandson. Every time my little Virginia got pregnant I would wish for a boy so that maybe then she could stop bringing your children into the world. But the more she tried for a boy the more girls kept coming. I love my granddaughters. But couldn't you manage to shoot out one boy? It's not up to the woman, you know. It's all on the man."

"Damn it, Ben, we get the children God sends us," cried Fonzi. "Get off my back!"

Colton liked both of them. They reminded him of his dad and his uncle Tad who never got along. But after his father's death his uncle Tad had been the one to give the eulogy and there hadn't been a dry eye in the church when he was done.

During dinner, Colton sat between Lauren and Virginia. The dining room table was laden with Southern cuisine that Virginia had modified to make healthier for her family. She never fried anything, or used fatty pork to season her greens. She used smoked turkey instead. Her menu today included baked chicken, mustard greens, sweet potato soufflé, macaroni and cheese, acre peas with whole okra and corn muffins. For dessert she'd made a golden cake with chocolate icing, Fonzi's favorite.

Everyone ate to their heart's content. Benjamin, though a small man, put away a prodigious amount of food. After he'd finished eating, he burped loudly. "Excuse me," he said sheepishly. "You know, in some cultures that's a sign you enjoyed the meal, and I did, baby girl. Everything was delicious, but now I should be getting on the road. It's a long drive back home."

"Won't you stay another night, Dad?" Virginia said in cajoling tones.

"I'm sorry, I can't," Ben said regrettably.

His son-in-law was smiling happily. "Now, Ginny, he says he's got to be back by tomorrow morning to welcome some new guests. Let him go."

Ben ignored him. Instead, he turned his attention to Amina. "Mina, I know you're feeling at loose ends after coming back home. I'd like you to consider coming to work with me. I don't have anyone to leave the business to. Your mother, as you know, is my only child and you girls my only grandchildren. Your sisters have careers. Maybe owning a lodge would suit you. You never know. Want to give it a try?"

Mina was stunned because, number one, her grandfather hardly ever made grand gestures. He was too taciturn for long speeches. And number two, because he was always lamenting the fact that he didn't have a grandson, someone he could leave the lodge to when he died.

She got up and went to hug him. "Grandpa, I'd love to give it a try. In fact, I'll go throw a few things in my duffel bag and I'll leave with you right now. I'll do the driving."

"You can drive a stick shift?"

"Grandpa, I can drive anything with wheels," said Mina with a broad grin.

Her sisters, as excited as she was by their grandfather's offer, got up and followed her out of the dining room to help her pack.

Lauren kissed Colton's cheek before she joined her sisters, "Be back soon, sweetie."

Colton was left at the table with her parents and grandfather. Virginia smiled at him. "Things happen quickly around here."

Chapter 10

Lauren rarely phoned to make an appointment to inspect the building site of the children's hospital. She liked to drop by unexpectedly, which served two purposes. It lessened the chance that she would run into Adam, and it also kept the construction crew on their toes.

It was a Friday in mid-February. The sun was shining brightly when Lauren arrived at the site at half past eleven. She was dressed in a dark gray pantsuit and comfortable heels. Because this was routine for her, she had brought her own hard hat that she had put on as soon as she got out of the car across the street from the site. The building's substructure or foundation had been completed and the crew had begun on the ground level.

She was spotted by one of the construction workers as soon as she walked onto the site and heard him
yell, "Hey, boss, the architect's here."

She smiled. They had a warning system. The foreman, whom she knew from her previous visits, was
a short, burly red-faced man in his forties with huge
biceps and a broad chest. He hurried toward her, smiling. "Miss Gaines. How are you today?"

"Hello, Mr. McPherson. Fine, thank you, and you?"

"Right as rain!" he said with a smile.

"I'm just going to do a quick walk-through if it's
all right with you," Lauren said casually. Specifically,
she was there to make certain the materials they were
using were of the highest quality and the skill with
which they applied them was up to par. "If you like,
you're free to join me," she told him. She didn't want
to put anyone's teeth on edge. She tried to make these
inspections as painless for the crew as possible. If she
saw shoddy materials being used, for example, she
wouldn't put the blame on them but on their employer.

Bobby McPherson nodded his agreement. "I'd be
happy to."

"This is on a spread foundation, am I right?" she
asked Bobby.

"Yes, ma'am," he said. "Reinforced concrete isn't
as solid a foundation as a solid rock foundation but
this baby will stand the test of time."

She asked him for dimensions and he supplied
them. She walked the length of the foundation while
around her workers were bolting together steel beams,
girders and columns which would form the superstruc-

ture. The bolting was temporary. Workers would weld the steel together permanently later on.

After half an hour Lauren was satisfied with her walk-through and shook Bobby's hand as she prepared to leave.

"Looks good," she said. "Thank you, Mr. McPherson."

"Anytime, Miss Gaines," Bobby said as he walked alongside her. He scrunched up his face. "Um, ma'am, do you mind if I ask you a personal question?"

Lauren's brows rose in surprise. Bobby McPherson had never tried to delay her leaving. On the contrary, he always seemed relieved when she exited the site. She couldn't see any harm in him asking her a question, though, so she signaled for him to continue. "No, go ahead."

"Is it true you used to be married to the boss?"

"Yes, it's true," Lauren said easily.

His face reddened further. "Sorry, I don't mean to be nosy. It's just that you go by the name Gaines."

"I went back to using my maiden name after the divorce," she said feeling a bit uncomfortable explaining this to Adam's foreman. It was apparent, though, that Adam had told Bobby McPherson about their past relationship. The question was why had he taken the time to do that?

She got her answer when she started walking back across the street to her car. Adam was waiting next to it, smiling. Bobby McPherson must have phoned him or sent a text message before coming to meet her.

"Surprise inspection?" he asked, his light brown eyes alight with humor.

Lauren removed her hard hat and held it in front of her. "You know how it is. It's my job to make sure the customer gets the building he's paying for."

"Is everything to your satisfaction?"

"So far, so good," she said lightly.

"What are you doing for lunch?" he asked. "It's practically noon. Want to go to that café we used to like near here?"

"No, Adam, I don't want to share a meal with you," she said bluntly. Her eyes met his. "Look into my eyes. Do I show any indication that I'm the least bit interested in having a personal relationship with you?"

"It's a woman's right to change her mind," Adam said hopeful. "I can't imagine that Riley's giving you something I couldn't give you if you let me."

"I'm not going to discuss my relationship with Colton with you."

Adam frowned. "Relationship," he said dismissively. "You've only known him for six weeks."

"How do you know how long I've known him?" she asked suspiciously.

"I've asked around," he said hesitantly. "Okay, I hired a private detective to find out how you met. It was in the mountains during a snowstorm. I should never have given you that cabin."

Lauren laughed. "You didn't want it."

"If I'd known you would turn it into a love nest for you and Riley, I never would have given it to you."

Lauren wanted to go but he was standing right

in front of the driver's side door, blocking her from reaching for the door's handle. "I'm really tired of your games," she said with a long-suffering sigh. "You don't want me. You just don't want Colton to have me. Your possessions were always more important to you than I ever was."

"I already admitted that," Adam reminded her. "Okay, so you don't want me back. I get it. My question is, did you ever love me? If you did, you would have loved me unconditionally. You would have had it in your heart to forgive my transgressions."

"I'm not a saint," Lauren said. "I don't have it in me to keep forgiving someone for their transgressions, especially if those transgressions involve having sex with other women. Sex is supposed to be sacred. It doesn't mean the same when you're sharing your man."

"Is the sex that good with Riley?" He sounded as though any minute now he was going to start yelling.

"Did you not hear me when I said I wasn't going to discuss my relationship with Colton with you?" she asked incredulously.

"Of course I heard you, Lauren. I hear everything you say. I simply refuse to accept it. When we met you were totally innocent. I was your first."

"What has that got to do with anything?"

"You saved yourself for your husband," he said reasonably. "You believed that we would be together forever. I disappointed you and broke our bond. In some ways it broke you, too. Admit that, at least."

"I admit it," she readily said. "You broke my heart. That's why I'm not letting you near it again."

"I'm trying to restore your perfect dream," he said, his voice soft and sincere. "Your mother and father have had a long marriage. Your grandfather had been married to your grandmother for over fifty years when he lost her. So what if we had a hiccup in our marriage? We could remarry and continue the family tradition. Riley can't offer you that, he's no better than I *was*. He's a playboy. Eventually he'll grow tired of you and move on to the next beautiful woman. Could his feelings for you be anything other than lust? Maybe he's a little grateful to you for saving his life. The detective said he would have probably frozen to death if you hadn't let him in. Lust and gratefulness are all your relationship is based on. Do you know what an orgasm is? It's a chemical reaction in the body. Oxytocin, called the love hormone, is released when you climax. People mistake it for love and before you know it you're in a relationship. Think about that. You and I have a history. He's only a hormone releaser in a good-looking package," he concluded.

"Wow," said Lauren, shaking her head in awe. "You are such a silver-tongued devil I'm almost convinced you're right, that Colton is just a handsome plaything. Fortunately, I'm immune to your lies and manipulation. Now get out of my way."

She went to reach around him for the door's handle and he pulled her into his arms and tried to kiss her. She dropped the hard hat and struggled against him. She hesitated using karate on him because at her present level of anger she might seriously injure him. So she gritted her teeth and pushed him hard in the chest, putting her weight into it, until he fell backward onto the pavement.

Adam laughed as he looked up at her from the ground. "I suppose I should be happy you didn't kick me in the crotch." He got to his feet and dusted himself off. "Sorry, darling. I was desperate to show you how I feel."

Lauren stood with her hands on her hips, her legs spread in a defiant stance. "Stop calling me *darling,* and I don't care if you're sincere about wanting me back. I don't want you. So I'm telling you, once and for all, leave me alone."

Adam's demeanor instantly changed. He'd been smiling ruefully. Now his eyes narrowed and his expression became mean and calculating. "You know I hate ultimatums. If you don't want me then let's see how long your lover boy will want you after he sees you in action."

"What do you mean by that?" Seeing her in action? Then it occurred to her. He was referring to compromising photos. She laughed because she had never in her life posed for any. He'd tried to cajole her into making a sex tape of the two of them just for their private viewing but she'd balked at it. And there had been no snapping of nude photos, either. She wasn't going to be caught all over the internet in her birthday suit.

"You can't be implying that you have compromising photos of me," she said indignantly. "I never agreed to do that with you."

"That doesn't mean I didn't film us together," he said with a smirk. "Remember the night we christened our new house? We made love in front of the fire. Your body looks so good in firelight. That film makes very fine viewing."

That was when she slugged him. It wasn't a karate move, it was an old-fashioned right cross to the jaw and it took him by surprise. His head snapped to the side and there was a sharp cracking sound. Lauren thought she'd broken his jaw and for one fleeting moment, wished she had. But when he looked at her again, his eyes watering, his hand gingerly touching his face, she saw that his jaw was intact.

He blinked at her as though his vision might not be clear. "Damn, you put some power behind that punch. I used to think you were exaggerating when you said you took martial arts from a young age, but that really hurt."

"Boss, boss, are you okay!" Bobby McPherson shouted as he came running across the street with two other men in tow.

"I'm fine, Bobby," Adam said. "No need for your concern. Please go back to work."

Bobby looked from him to Lauren. "Are you sure? She still looks mad to me."

"Yes, I'm sure," Adam said decisively.

Bobby reluctantly backed away and gestured to the two men who'd arrived with him to head back across the street to the site.

Alone with Lauren again, Adam said, "That's going

to cost you. I have witnesses who'll testify that you assaulted me.

"Now, I'm going to tell you what you're going to do. You're going to stop seeing Riley. After which you're going to come back to me."

"You're delusional," Lauren said, her voice harsh. She was shaking the kinks out of the hand she'd hit him with. The pain was subsiding. "I'm not doing anything without proof that you really do have a sex tape."

He calmly reached into his inside coat pocket and retrieved a small videotape.

She couldn't believe he was producing the tape at this very moment. "You meant to provoke me from the beginning," she accused, livid. "You were prepared for this outcome."

He smiled cockily. "I'm a son of a bitch. That has been well established over the years. Too bad you didn't remember that when you started giving me ultimatums." He pressed the tape into her hand. "Enjoy the show."

He turned to leave.

"What if I call your bluff and tell Colton you're trying to blackmail me?"

He looked her in the eye. "You wouldn't do that. You'd be afraid he'd try to kill me and you wouldn't want his spending the rest of his life in prison on your conscience."

"Don't be too confident that you have me where you want me," Lauren warned.

Adam grinned. "I'll take my chances."

He left then, not glancing back. She stood there

frozen, watching his retreating back and wondering what she'd ever done to deserve this.

Lauren drove around for a while, not wanting to go back to the office because she knew she wouldn't be able to concentrate on work while she had the tape in her possession. So she phoned the office, and when Meredith answered she told her she wasn't feeling well and wouldn't be in for the rest of the afternoon. She didn't have any appointments today, but asked that Meredith please inform the partners of her plans if they inquired about her in her absence.

At home, she put the tape in and pressed Play. Seeing her and Adam making love should have been old hat, but it made her sick to her stomach that she'd ever given herself to him. There was nothing particularly kinky about their lovemaking session on the night they'd christened their new home. If Colton actually looked at it, how would he react? No one wanted to see the person they were involved with making love to someone else. She knew she would be mortified if she saw a sex tape with Colton and another woman. Would it force him to quit seeing her?

Lauren sat on the couch thinking, torturing herself, working out several scenarios in her head. She couldn't allow Adam to manipulate her. That was a given. The question was, how was she going to beat him at his own game?

Maybe she could break into his house and steal the tape. But the problem with that was he might have copies hidden elsewhere. Perhaps in a safety deposit box or in a wall safe in his house. He could have even given a copy to a friend to hold on to for him.

Then something occurred to her. It was illegal to tape someone without their knowledge, wasn't it? She picked up her cell phone and quickly dialed her lawyer's number.

"Arielle Maxey's office," the secretary said brightly. "How can I help you?"

"Is Arielle in?" Lauren asked.

"I'm sorry, Miss Maxey's in a meeting. May I give her a message for you?"

"This is Lauren Gaines. Please tell Arielle to phone me as soon as possible. My ex-husband is trying to blackmail me."

There was a sharp intake of breath and an exhale on the other end of the line followed by a quick "I'll give her the message right away, Miss Gaines."

"Thank you," Lauren said and then hung up.

Lauren pointed the remote at the video tape player and switched it off. She was breathing a bit easier now. Having taken some kind of action instead of simply panicking had made her feel better.

Fifteen minutes later, Arielle phoned.

"What's this I hear about Adam trying to blackmail you?" she asked belligerently. Arielle, in her midthirties, was a sister who seemed to be always itching for a fight. Lauren thought she was well-suited for her profession.

Lauren explained what was going on and waited patiently while Arielle sat silent on the other end of the line for a couple of minutes. Arielle didn't like to blurt out responses. She was a thinker, a ruminator. Consequently, her responses were sometimes long and drawn out, although very thorough and logical.

"You say you had no knowledge whatsoever that you were being recorded?"

"That's something I would never agree to," Lauren assured her. "Not in this day and age."

"Oh, yes, I have several clients who have regretted letting their lovers or spouses tape them in compromising positions. Blackmail is often a part of it. They threaten to put it on the internet or send it to someone unless you do what they say. There are some sick puppies out there.

"In the state of North Carolina taping someone without their knowledge isn't illegal if the taping is being done in a public place where there is no prior expectation of privacy. But in your home where you didn't give your permission, and you can expect to have your privacy respected, it is most definitely illegal. Maybe Adam should have consulted his lawyer before trying to strong-arm you into doing his bidding. Do you want me to call him and threaten him with prosecution? It would be my pleasure to do so."

"No, wait, I have more questions," Lauren told her. "Can I sue him for all the copies of the tape?"

"We can try," Arielle told her. "But it's highly unlikely that we would find all the copies. He would probably lie about it. I think you should tell Colton what's going on and warn him that Adam has threatened to send the tape to him. He can then choose to destroy the tape before watching it."

"Do you really think it'll be that easy?" Lauren asked skeptically. "I like him a lot, Arielle. I don't want to lose him over this."

"He's a mature adult," Arielle said. "He knows that you and Adam had a sex life."

"Yes, but what if he doesn't destroy the tape and watches it? Once you see something like that it's etched in your memory. I'm in it and it disgusts me."

Arielle laughed shortly. "Because Adam disgusts you," she pointed out.

"Yes, that's true. But if the shoe were on the other foot, I wouldn't want to see Colton with another woman."

"My advice is still to tell him what's going on so he'll be prepared in case Adam sends it to him out of spite after you tell him to go to hell. You're going to tell him to go to hell, aren't you?"

"Yes, and threaten him with jail if he ever shows that tape to anyone!" Lauren exclaimed, getting to her feet. She had decided that there was no time like the present. "In fact, I'm going over there right now and tell him to his face."

"No more hitting," Arielle warned. "He could still press charges against you for assault."

"No more hitting," Lauren promised. "Thanks, Arielle."

"My pleasure," said Arielle.

Chapter 11

It only took fifteen minutes for Lauren to reach the Eckhart Construction building on Atlantic Avenue. When she walked into the office the receptionist, a gorgeous young African American woman with silky straight hair falling nearly to her waist, inquired why she was there. Lauren wondered where Edie was. Edie had been the receptionist for years and Lauren had liked her.

Forcing a smile, Lauren said, "Tell Mr. Eckhart his ex-wife is here."

As if she suspected Lauren was there to cause a scene, a panicked expression crossed the woman's face but soon vanished and was replaced by a polite smile. "I'm sorry, but Mr. Eckhart isn't here."

Lauren hadn't expected this. Adam was a workaholic. He was always at the office unless he was on-site somewhere.

"Then he's visiting one of his sites?" she asked, her tone friendly but insistent.

"I'm not at liberty to give out that information," the receptionist replied stiffly.

Irritated now, Lauren narrowed her eyes. "Look, I just want to talk to him."

"I'm sorry," the receptionist said again, her voice rising. "Please leave before I have someone escort you off the premises."

Suddenly, Edie came walking swiftly into the outer office, a look of concern on her mocha-colored face. Heading straight for Lauren, she cried, "Mrs. Eckhart, what a lovely surprise."

Smiling, she reached for Lauren's hand and they shook. Lauren breathed a sigh of relief. "Finally, a friendly face," she said.

Edie didn't immediately let go of her hand but led her back to her office. Lauren saw from the sign on the door that she'd been promoted to office manager.

Edie closed the door behind them and then hugged Lauren. They were old friends, after all, and she'd missed her. "It's wonderful to see you. How've you been?"

"I'm doing well," Lauren said with a warm smile. "How are you and yours?"

"Oh, the family's healthy and that's what counts," Edie said. In her early forties, Edie was of average weight and height, had light brown skin and dark brown eyes and wore her shoulder-length brown hair in a straight style with bangs. "As for me, I'm over-worked and underpaid, as usual."

They laughed. Once their laughter subsided, Edie met Lauren's eyes and said, "I assume you're look-ing for Adam?"

"Yes, do you know where he is?"

"He came in here a few minutes ago and went to his office but then he came back out and said he was going home. He was in some pain and thought taking something for it and lying down would help."

Lauren panicked. Did she hit him harder than she thought she had? Maybe he had a concussion. If so, he shouldn't take any medication or go to sleep. That could be asking for trouble. "Okay," she said to Edie, trying her best to appear as though she was in no real rush to leave but desperately wanting to run out. "I guess I'll try him at the house, then. Thanks, Edie." She gave Edie another quick hug. "Take care of your-self, and congrats on the promotion."

"Thanks," Edie said, smiling but looking at her strangely. She walked with her to the exit. "You're feeling okay, aren't you?"

"Oh, yes, yes, I'm fine," Lauren said.

Once on the other side of the door she sprinted to her car. She had to remind herself not to speed as she drove across town to the exclusive neighborhood where her former home was located. It would be fool-ish to speed and risk being pulled over by a police of-ficer. A delay might be the difference between life and death.

As she drove she remembered when she got up this

morning and looked out her window and thought that this was such a beautiful day. She'd been eager to get it started. Now she wished it was over. Why had she hit him? He'd provoked her, true. But all her life she'd been trained not to hit anyone unless in self-defense or in the defense of someone incapable of defending themselves. Yet she'd violently attacked Adam because he'd said something that angered her. So many times people did things in anger that they were unable to take back. If he died because she lacked anger management skills she would have to live with the consequences for the rest of her life.

She made record time getting to the house on Cone Manor Lane.

The stone Tudor Revival home had been built five years ago. Adam had had it built as a surprise for their first wedding anniversary so she had not had any say in its design. Although a beautiful home, she found it too big and ostentatious. She would have preferred a less cavernous house with personal details that made you feel at home when you stepped into its foyer. This house was two stories tall with a sweeping staircase. It had five bedrooms, five full baths and two half baths. It boasted almost eight thousand square feet of usable space and sat on two acres. There was a pool out back, and a gym and a home theater in the basement. It was an estate, not a house. Adam liked living large.

She got out of the Range Rover and ran to the front door. She was about to ring the bell when she noticed the door was ajar. She paused. Adam would not leave the door unlocked. He was usually careful about security.

Her mind racing, she tried to think what she should do, quietly enter the house and check things out firsthand? Or go ahead and phone the police? If she phoned the police and nothing was amiss she'd look like a fool. But looking like a fool was preferable to walking in and finding Adam dead on the floor from the knock on the head she'd given him. She didn't think she could handle discovering a dead body, even if that dead body belonged to her horrible ex-husband.

Unfortunately, while she was mentally debating what her next move should be, a dark figure approached the door holding a gun in her hand and demanded she enter the house.

Lauren grimaced when she saw the business end of the .38 pointing at her and then slowly raised her gaze to look into the face of her assailant, Nichole Kelly.

"I thought I heard a car pull up. You're just the woman I want to see," said Nichole as she backed into the house, gun trained on Lauren. "Come with me, and don't make any sudden moves. You and I need to talk."

After they were inside, Nichole said, "Lock the door."

Lauren did as she was told.

Nichole went to her and shoved her farther into the house. "We're going to his office," she said, her voice calm but decisive. In the office, a large luxuriously furnished room replete with a custom-built stone fireplace, Lauren saw that Adam had been duct-taped to a chair and his mouth was sealed shut.

She wondered how Nichole had managed that. Adam must have weighed a hundred pounds more than she did. Then when she got closer to him she saw that he had a bloody gash on the back of his head. She certainly hadn't done that. She'd struck him on the jaw. Nichole must have snuck up behind him and hit him with a blunt object.

Adam had apparently been sitting in his office chair when she'd hit him from behind and while he was unconscious she'd gone to work on him with a roll of duct tape.

Lauren turned and faced Nichole. "What's going on here? Why is he trussed up like that?"

"Because I decided not to kill him right away," Nichole said. Her eyes were bright and there was a crazed expression in them.

Lauren was pretty sure her own eyes were bright, too, with desperation. She didn't want to get shot.

"All right," Lauren said slowly. "What did you want to talk with me about?"

"First," said Nichole, "what are you doing here? And don't lie to me because I'm upset and I don't want to have to shoot you."

"I don't want you to shoot me," Lauren said with a nervous smile. "I'm here because he and I argued and I hauled off and hit Adam earlier today and when I went to his office to talk with him I was told that he'd gone home in pain. I was worried that if he had a concussion from the punch I threw, he could possibly die."

"So you came to see if he was okay," Nichole concluded for her.

Lauren nodded. "Yes."

"Why did you hit him?"

"Because he threatened to show a sex tape he'd made of us while we were married to the guy I'm seeing now unless I agreed to come back to him."

Nichole said, "Huh?"

"Do I have to repeat that? He was trying to blackmail me."

"He told me you two were still in love," Nichole said, "And because of that he had to dump me." She lowered the gun as she talked and paced the floor.

Lauren glanced at Adam who was conscious and trying his best to follow Nichole with his eyes. He reminded her of a horse with a bit in its mouth, eyes rolling from side to side. She wondered if he really did have a concussion. He'd been hit on the head by angry women twice today.

"I guess he'd forgotten he gave me the alarm code and a key to the house after we got engaged. I had planned on coming in while he was away and getting my few personal belongings as I did one day last week. But when I was here I discovered his little hobby. He has about fifty videotapes of himself and several women having sex. He labels them with the first letter of the name of his conquests. He had ten in there with the letter *N*. He had around twenty with the letter *L*."

"You bastard," Lauren cried angrily, glaring at Adam. "You only showed me one."

"I was so upset I left that day without remembering to get the belongings I'd come for," Nichole continued. "So I came back today for them and he picked today of all days to come home early from work. He never does that. I hid while he came in here and sat down at his desk. I was so angry with him for taping me without my permission that I hit him over the head with his own gun. You probably know the one he keeps in his desk drawer?"

Lauren shook her head nervously.

Nichole smiled. "You're okay."

"Thank you," Lauren said with a smile. "I thought you were very nice the first time we met. I wondered why you were with him."

"I'm sure many people thought the same thing when you were with him," Nichole returned the compliment.

Adam mumbled loudly as if he were reminding them to get back on topic. They both glared at him.

"Now I'm contemplating whether I should just off him or humiliate him."

"I vote for humiliation," Lauren said. "Death is final and mercifully quick. Humiliation on the other hand lasts a lifetime."

Nichole cocked her brow, her interest piqued. "What do you suggest we do?"

Adam protested even louder.

"Shut up, we're trying to think," said Lauren. "Mmm, what would be a fitting punishment for a pig like him?"

"We should definitely destroy his videotape collection," she told Nichole.

"Of course," Nichole agreed. She went over to an antique armoire inside which sat a flat-screen TV and bent down to open the bottom drawer. "They're all in here."

"We can burn them in the fireplace," Lauren said. "And make him watch."

In a matter of minutes they had a fire going in the fireplace and were tossing the videotapes into it. They talked while they tossed.

"You know," said Nichole. "When we met I was prepared not to like you. He talked about you like you were Satan's daughter. How you never supported him. You wouldn't quit your job to entertain his clients. To think I was preparing to quit my job."

"Oh, no," Lauren said. "You should never give up your career for a man. If he's a real man he wouldn't want you to give up something that means so much to you."

Nichole tossed a videotape with the letter N on it into the fire. "I'm glad I didn't quit. Where would I be now? I'd be out of a job with no way to pay my bills."

"What do you do?" Lauren asked.

"I'm a massage therapist," Nichole said. "That's how we met. I gave him a massage. I should have known he was no good when he asked me if I could please him with my hands. But I thought he was just flirting. I'm a certified massage therapist. These fingers are for healing, not for giving happy endings."

After they'd put all of the tapes into the fire, they turned their attention to Adam once more.

"I think we should videotape him in his present state and keep copies for ourselves as a guarantee that he won't try to seek revenge for what we're doing to him," Lauren suggested.

Nichole wrinkled her nose, thinking about it. "Okay, let's do that. But I also have an idea."

"I'm all ears," said Lauren.

"We can't unbind him," Nichole said. "He's strong. He may be able to overpower us. Maybe we could cut the clothes off him and film him using that expensive camcorder of his. And after we're finished we could roll him outside and leave him naked and taped to his chair on the front lawn."

Adam really started yelling then. However, with the tape over his mouth the sound was muffled and didn't carry very far.

Lauren laughed. "I wish we could do that, but there's no way to cut his clothes off him while he's duct-taped to that chair. We're going to have to leave him where he is and call 911 on the way out. He's been hit on the head twice. He might need medical attention."

Nichole looked in the middle distance for a few seconds then said, "Yeah, you're right." She glared at Adam. "You're not having a fun day are you, sweetheart?"

Shortly after that, the partners in crime got busy. Lauren filmed Adam as he thrashed around in the wheeled office chair, trying his best to hide his face from the camera. Once she had a few minutes of footage she removed the tape and put another in so that they would each have a copy. Nichole wiped down all surfaces that might have their fingerprints on them.

Lastly, she wiped the gun down and returned it to the desk drawer.

Finished, the two women stood facing one another. Lauren offered Nichole her hand to shake. "I'm sorry things didn't work out well for you. You seem like a nice person."

"Ditto," Nichole said, smiling. "Do you want to call 911, or should I?"

"I'll do it," Lauren said. She picked up the phone on Adam's desk and dialed. When the dispatcher asked what the nature of her emergency was, she said, "This guy brought me home with him and he started getting rough with me. I hit him and tied him up. I think I might have hit him too hard. I'm outta here!" She then hung up the phone. "Since this is his house phone. They'll know exactly where to come," she explained to Nichole.

Lauren reached into her coat pocket and removed a business card. She gave it to Nichole. "We're connected now. Here's my contact information."

Nichole's face lit up. "I don't have a card," she said regrettably. She walked over to Adam's desk and borrowed a pad and pen to write down her address and phone number. Walking back over to Lauren, she gave her a slip of paper and said, "Who knows, one day we might get together over drinks and reminisce."

Lauren smiled at that. "Stranger things have happened."

Then they left Adam where he sat and vacated the premises. Outside, Lauren waved to Nichole as they both hurried to their vehicles.

* * *

Too keyed-up to go home, Lauren drove around awhile, relishing the fact that she was finally rid of Adam. He no longer had the means with which to blackmail her, unless Nichole was wrong and she had not discovered his entire stash of videotapes. However, she had a good feeling they'd destroyed all of them. And there was nothing left to come back to haunt her.

While driving she put in a follow-up call to Arielle. Arielle answered her personal number. "Hey, Lauren," she said, "I don't have to come get you out of jail, do I?"

Lauren laughed and told her what had happened.

When she was finished relating the tale, Arielle said, "You must really care about Colton Riley to do all this to prevent him from seeing those tapes."

Lauren did care about Colton very much. What she felt for him was hard to put into words. "I don't know if it was out of the humiliation I felt for being secretly recorded or my fear that if I let Adam get away with what he planned that I would always be subject to his whims. I got away from him once. I wasn't going back there again."

"I'm just glad the police didn't get involved," Arielle told her. "If Adam knows what's good for him he'll keep quiet about it. But if he does decide to raise a big stink and report you and Nichole, you don't have any evidence that you were provoked to do what you did. You burned all the tapes."

Lauren patted her coat pocket. She felt the two small rectangular objects she'd secured earlier. "No," she told her lawyer. "I didn't destroy them all. I kept one with an *N* and one with an *L*. I'll send Nichole hers tomorrow and explain why I kept it."

"I knew some of my smarts would rub off on you eventually." Arielle laughed a good ten seconds, then said, "So, none of your actions had anything to do with Mr. Riley?"

"I already told you I didn't want to lose him because of Adam's treachery," Lauren said.

"Are you going to tell him what you did?"

"Yes, I can't take the chance that Adam will be vindictive in spite of everything and tell him about the tapes just to hurt him."

"He doesn't play well with others, our Adam," Arielle said wisely.

"I'm going to try Colton now and see if he's available to talk," Lauren said. "Thanks again, Arielle."

"You take care," Arielle said and disconnected the call.

Chapter 12

Colton had just come out of a meeting with the company's accountants when he received Lauren's call. He was happy to hear from her and told her so. "You've been on my mind all day," he said, his voice husky with longing.

"You've been on my mind, too," she said, "Something's happened and I need to talk to you. Can you spare a few minutes?"

"Sure," he answered without hesitation. "Where are you? I can either come to you or you could come here."

"I'm not too far from you," Lauren said. "I'll be there in ten minutes."

"This must be important." A hint of worry was apparent in his voice. "You're not in any trouble?"

"I was," she said softly, "I think the problem's solved but you should still know about it."

"All right," said Colton. "I'm here for you."

The Riley Construction Company offices were downtown. Lauren had a hard time finding a parking space and wound up taking longer than ten minutes to get there. When she walked into Colton's office, he breathed a sigh of relief and pulled her into his arms, kicking the door closed. They hadn't seen each other since Wednesday when Colton had cooked for her at his place. The workweek kept them busy and the time between their next meeting felt agonizingly long.

He gazed down into her upturned face. He was wearing dark gray dress slacks and a long-sleeved light blue dress shirt, its sleeves rolled up, and black wing tips. His suit jacket hung from a coat tree in the corner. He'd removed the tie earlier in the day. As he peered into her eyes, he drank her in. Her widely spaced eyes were smoky with desire and he was happy he was the one who put that expression in them.

"God, I've missed you," he said breathlessly and lowered his head to kiss her sweet mouth.

Lauren had missed him, too, and returned his kiss with fervor. She moaned softly, relishing the delicious taste and feel of his mouth on hers, the slow, deliberate, extremely sexy havoc his tongue wreaked on hers. She felt the kiss down to her toes. She looked into his eyes when they parted and reached up to caress his strong jaw. *I did do it for him,* she thought, astonished. Arielle was right. In that instant, she knew that she would have done anything not to lose him. Adam's threat had thrown her into protective mode. She had thought she was protecting herself and doing what she'd always done, which was solve her own problems.

She realized now that she always wanted Colton to look at her in the manner he was looking at her right now: with admiration, longing and sensual intensity. She believed that if he had seen those tapes, he would never have looked at her in the same way again. Therefore, she'd gone with her gut and tried her best to put Adam in his place.

Her hand still on his jaw, she said softly, her gaze locked with his, "It's been quite a day."

She told him everything from the beginning. Her fight with Adam on the street, what had happened when she'd gotten to his house, and the burning of the tapes except for the couple she'd saved for insurance.

His gray eyes were riveted on her face. A frown creased his brow. His inner turmoil was evident from the pained expression in his gray depths. "Why didn't you call me?" he asked, his jaw muscles clenching in obvious irritation. "You could have been hurt going to his house like that. What if Nichole had been convinced that you were the reason he'd dumped her? What if she had shot you in a jealous rage?"

Lauren reached out and touched his cheek to soothe him, but he drew away from her. "Lauren, I think you take your independence too far," he said, his eyes narrowed in anger. "It never occurred to you to call somebody? Myself, your father or your sisters? Your first reaction was to phone your lawyer."

"For legal advice," she said in her defense. "You or my father or my sisters couldn't give me that."

"No, but one of us would have talked you out of going over to Eckhart's house after you'd hit him."

"I was afraid he'd suffered a concussion," she cried. "I had to make sure I hadn't injured him too badly. Believe me when I tell you I took no pleasure in setting foot on Cone Manor Lane again."

He sighed heavily. "You're so stubborn. You should have called me. You think that because you've got a black belt in karate and know how to use a handgun, you're invulnerable, some kind of superwoman. You're not. You foolishly risked your life today."

"I had no way of knowing what I was going to walk into when I went to his house."

"That's my point," Colton ground out. He took a deep breath in an attempt to calm down. "Why did you do it? I know you have better sense than to trust Eckhart. Why didn't you call his bluff? I wouldn't have watched that tape for anything in the world. The last thing I want to see is Eckhart making love to you."

"I know that," Lauren said as if that proved her point. "That's why I had to make sure you never got the chance to."

"You still should have called," he repeated.

"What would you have done if I had?" she asked.

"I probably would have strangled him," Colton admitted, teeth bared in a snarl.

"That's why I didn't call you."

"I don't need your protection," he practically shouted but reeled it in because his secretary was in the outer office and he didn't want his and Lauren's business all over the office.

"And I don't need yours," Lauren countered fiercely. "It's true, I'm independent. It's the only way I know how to be. Adam threatened to send you the tape he showed me unless I broke things off with you. I did what I thought was the right thing. I fought back."

"You would have done better by dumping me," Colton told her angrily.

Lauren saw red. "Okay, consider yourself dumped!" Arms crossed over her chest, she stubbornly turned her back to him.

Colton laughed. "There's that stubborn streak again."

"I'm serious," Lauren insisted, turning back around to face him. "I'm here to tell you we can't see each other anymore. I'm obviously too far gone on you for my own good if I would do anything in my power not to lose you. So, let's call it quits, shall we? It's probably the best thing for both of us."

"You can't quit me," Colton told her angrily. They were standing facing one another in front of his desk. She was so upset her chest was heaving.

"I most certainly can," Lauren begged to differ. Her eyes bored into his. "Apparently, what we have between us is a chemical reaction."

"If that's how you look when you're getting ready to dump me, with your breasts about to burst out of your blouse, you're not very convincing," Colton said, "because you know that chemical combustion you mentioned only happens between you and me. It's unique. Stop making it sound trivial. I got angry because I was scared that I might have lost you due to the fact that you're so stubbornly independent you couldn't call me when you got into trouble. That pisses me off. I'm a man and a man has to feel needed. We are cavemen in that respect. Got that? It's our duty to protect our women. Superwomen like you don't understand that, or don't want to understand it. Your father loved you but he did you a disservice when he taught you to be so remarkably self-sufficient. If you ever do anything as foolish as you did today, you won't have to quit me. I'll be forced to let you go." Then he roughly pulled her into his embrace and kissed her hard. He kept the kiss intact until she fell limply into his arms.

After they came up for air she looked up dreamily at him. "You win this round. I'd better go."

She reluctantly left his warm embrace and turned to leave.

"Are you capable of driving?" he teased with a broad grin.

"Shut up," she said as she walked to the door on wobbly legs.

Colton had every intention of letting it go. The remainder of his workday he tried to put Adam Eckhart and what he'd done to Lauren out of his mind, but he hadn't been able to shake it, so he decided to have a man to man talk with him. It wasn't hard to track him down. He went to the closest hospital to Eckhart's home address. When he got there he tried the emergency room and, masquerading as Eckhart's brother, he learned that they were keeping him overnight for observation. Apparently, he'd taken a good beating. He found him asleep in a semiprivate room, the other bed occupied by an elderly man channel-surfing and mumbling about nothing being on TV.

When the guy looked up and saw Colton, he said, "Who're you looking for?"

"Adam Eckhart," said Colton.

"That's sleepyhead," Adam's roommate said. He laughed. "But if I'd been hit over the head like that I'd probably want to sleep, too."

Colton strode over to Adam's bed and loudly cleared his throat.

Adam startled awake. When he saw who was standing beside his bed, his eyes narrowed with hatred. "What the hell do you want?"

"Just checking to see if you were still alive," Colton said with a smile. "How does it feel to get your ass kicked by two women?"

Adam winced as he sat up in bed. The back of his head had a huge bandage on it and he was wearing a hospital gown. "Go ahead and issue your threat, Riley. I know that's why you're here. Lauren came running to you and now you're here to demonstrate what a big hero you are."

"No," Colton denied calmly. "I'm not going to threaten you. I'm going to make a promise to you. I vow that should you ever even look at Lauren funny I will put you in the ground, not the hospital." He smiled. "Are we clear?"

Adam didn't say anything. The color had drained from his face, and he felt dizzy. "I suppose it makes you feel better coming here and threatening me in my weakened state. I can't defend myself. But, yes, we are clear."

"Listen, if you'd like to revisit this when you're healthy again, you know where to find me," Colton offered. "I just wanted to state my case and be done with it. Trying to blackmail Lauren was despicable. But I'm sure you already know that. Plus, the fact that you taped unsuspecting women for your viewing pleasure is plain sleazy. It amazes me that a man as successful as you are can't find something better to do with his time. Seek help, Eckhart."

"I'm not a head case," Adam said, holding his head with both hands. "Get out!"

"I'd be happy to," Colton told him. "Just repeat what I said to make certain you understood me."

"Yeah, yeah, I'm not to ever go near Lauren again. I got it. Good riddance to her. She never appreciated the finer things in life. She wants to roll around in the gutter with the likes of you."

Colton laughed softly. "You're a piece of work, Eckhart."

"What, are you surprised I'm unrepentant? Was I supposed to cower and say I'm sorry for what I did? I'm just sorry it didn't succeed. I was looking forward to her starring in more of my home movies," Adam said with a smirk.

Colton almost hit him when he said that. Restraint was aided by the sudden appearance of a nurse who had come to take Adam's vitals.

Colton turned on his heels and left. He didn't know

if his talk with Eckhart had gotten through to him. He simply had wanted to make sure Eckhart knew that in the future he would be prepared to deal with him in a deadly and final manner should he resume his harassment of Lauren.

As the weeks passed, to Lauren's relief, she never ran into Adam when she visited the children's hospital site. He did phone her one day when she was on the way home from work. She'd looked at her cell phone's screen and seriously thought of not answering but she did because she wanted to know if he'd fully recovered from his head wounds.

"Yes, Adam, what do you want?"

"I'm surprised you answered," he said.

"Don't waste time making small talk."

"This is hard for me to say," he began almost timidly.

"Well, I have no trouble telling you to go to hell if you've called to make further threats. The fact is I saved your life. Nichole had snapped. She was going to shoot you. If I hadn't been there I don't know what would have happened."

"That's why I'm calling," Adam said, "To thank you for saving my life. I do believe Nichole hated me in that moment. She might have done something crazy."

"Yeah, yeah," Lauren said skeptically, "What's the catch?"

"No catch," Adam disavowed. "I'm not incapable of learning from my mistakes, you know. You don't have to worry about me anymore. No seeking revenge or any of that. I, um, I wish you the best."

At that point she was really suspicious. "What brought this on?"

"Almost dying can have a spiritual effect on a man," was all he said. "Goodbye, Lauren."

After hanging up Lauren had wondered if indeed Adam had changed. Only time would tell.

Nichole had phoned Lauren after she received the tape Lauren had sent to her. She'd had misgivings about destroying all of the evidence and was glad that Lauren had had the foresight not to. They had agreed to keep in touch.

Spring was soon upon them and Lauren and Colton planned a long weekend at her cabin to enjoy the season in the mountains. They set off early one Saturday morning in April in Colton's SUV.

"Grandpa Beck wants us to come to the lodge tonight for dinner," she told Colton as he drove. "Since Mina has been there he's becoming a lot more social. And she's transformed the lodge by adding a few decorative touches and bringing the place into the twenty-first century with internet connections. Could you believe he didn't offer Wi-Fi? She sent photos. His rustic lodge now appeals to a whole new clientele. Bookings have doubled. Grandpa Beck complains that they'll never have any downtime if things keep up like they have been lately."

"Good for him," Colton said.

Lauren laughed. "Mina says he complains all the time, but she can tell he's secretly pleased."

"What about Mina?" Colton asked. "Does she like living up there?"

"She loves it. It keeps her mind occupied, and Mina likes to stay extremely busy so she doesn't have to think too hard. When she thinks she invariably comes back to the fact that she lost the man she loved."

"That must be hard to forget no matter how much she works," said Colton.

"It is," said Lauren sadly. "But what else can she do but take one day at a time and continue living? She knows Keith would want her to find love again."

The day was bright and sunny. As they drew closer to the mountains the air got crisper. The leaves on the trees had turned from orange and yellow to green.

Colton had been looking forward to this weekend. Although he and Lauren tried to see each other at least once or twice each week, it was never enough time. Many of their weekends were spent with each other's families. There had been birthday parties, Sunday dinners and a big get-together to celebrate Lauren's parents' anniversary. He enjoyed getting to know her family. But what he really wanted was more alone time with her.

He glanced over at her. She was thumbing a text message to someone, her face scrunched up in concentration. Her long wavy hair was in a ponytail, and she was wearing well-worn jeans and a short-sleeved Duke University T-shirt. She'd kicked off her sandals miles back. She knew how to relax.

In fact, she was good at many things, including making him fall in love with her. It had been four months since they'd met on that fateful winter night.

He smiled as he returned his attention solely to his driving. He was remembering a conversation he'd had with his mother a couple days ago. She'd come by the office because she wanted to tell him that she was going back to work. For years she had been an interior decorator. His father would build the houses and she would design the interior of the model homes. His father often said that the houses he built were structurally sound and built to last, but if not for his mother's contribution no one touring them would see them as homes.

That day in his office, Colton had said, "Why would you want to go back to work? Dad left you financially secure. You don't ever have to work again. Why not enjoy life? Go to Paris. Run with the bulls in Pamplona. You can do anything you want to."

"Running with the bulls is a man thing," Veronica had said with a smile. "Besides, working is what I want to do, not be on a perennial vacation. I need purpose in my life. I need to contribute something to society."

"You're contributing something to society by being my mother," Colton said in response to her plea for purpose. "I still need you. Jade needs you. You've got two grandchildren to spoil. A lot of mothers would be trying to marry me off, and you're looking to go back to work."

"Honey, you're a hairbreadth away from fulfilling

your father's and my wishes for marrying you off," Veronica told him smugly.

That had gotten Colton's attention. He'd stood up behind his desk, rested his hands atop it and glared down at his mother who had the grace to squirm a little in her comfy leather chair across from him. "I know that tone," he began, his voice firm. "What do you know that I don't?"

"Darling, do you remember my telling you about that game your dad and I used to play? Whenever we'd meet a young lady we thought would suit you we'd say, could she be the girl for Colton? Well, Lauren was at the top of our list. Of course back then she was married to that horrible Eckhart man but we always held out hope. After your father died and you went to our cabin and had to spend time with Lauren I figured it was fate. I'm delighted that you and Lauren finally got together. I'm sure your father is somewhere laughing."

Colton had sat back down behind his desk, his eyes on his mother. Shaking his head in wonder, he said, "When were you planning on telling me this?"

"On your wedding day," said Veronica, smiling. "But since the wedding's on lock I'm telling you now."

"The wedding isn't on lock," Colton told her. "I haven't even told Lauren that I'm in love with her yet."

This put a look of concern on Veronica's face. "You don't love her?"

"Yes, I love her," Colton said out loud for the first time. "I love her but I'm trying to pick the right time to tell her. Lauren's experience with Eckhart left her heart bruised and battered. I don't think she's going to want to be in love anytime soon, even if she does love me."

"Huh?" said Veronica. "Speak English, please."

"Eckhart swept her off her feet," Colton explained. "Our relationship has been a whirlwind, too. How we met, the quick attraction—everything points to it being too soon to declare my love. She'll never take me seriously."

"You can't be sure of that unless you tell her," said his mother.

Now, as he drove toward Bryson City, Colton wondered exactly how he was going to convince Lauren that the love he felt for her was real and not infatuation or lust. At some point in a relationship built on lust a transition to love has to be made for the couple to stay together, right?

This weekend he resolved to let her know how much he loved her.

Chapter 13

"Oh, my God, girl, you look good!" Lauren exclaimed upon seeing Amina later that evening. She and Colton had driven over to Grandpa Beck's lodge after resting awhile then showering and dressing for dinner upon their arrival at her cabin.

Lauren had barely set foot out of the SUV before Amina hugged her tightly. "So do you," Amina said in her ear. "Being in love suits you."

The sisters both had on jeans and dressy blouses, but Lauren had on heels and Amina wore her trusty athletic shoes.

Lauren looked at her sister whose skin was glowing with good health. "I can't hide anything from you."

The lodge, a ten-thousand-square-foot three-story building made of hand-hewn pine logs stood in the midst of a pine forest. The lodge itself had eight guest rooms but there were also six small cabins dotting the property. Spring was Benjamin's busiest season even before Amina had become his partner. They were fully booked.

Her grandfather came out of the lodge and hugged her after Amina let her go. She stood eye to eye with him. "Grandpa, you remember Colton," Lauren said, gesturing to Colton who was coming around the SUV to shake Benjamin Beck's hand.

Ben looked up at Colton with a smile on his weathered face. "Sure, I do. How are you, Colton?"

"Just great, sir," said Colton. His gaze took in the charm of the lodge and the splendor of the surrounding woods. "This is quite a place you have here."

"Wait until you see the inside," said Benjamin proudly. All four of them began walking toward the two-story entrance of the lodge. Huge tree trunk columns stood sentinel on either side of the intricately carved door that reminded Colton of a totem pole. In the wood of the door there were images of forest animals and eagles soaring in the sky.

Inside the foyer the ceiling rose two stories, and a curved staircase led to the guest rooms. Pine floors polished to a high gleam stretched as far as the eye could see. A fireplace large enough to roast a pig in was the main focus of the lobby.

Heavy pine furnishings with beige cushions composed the seating groups near the fireplace and African and American Indian art in the form of wood sculptures and woven throws on the couches and chairs lent a Western charm to the décor.

"I like it," Lauren said appreciatively to her sister and grandfather after observing the touches Amina had added to the lodge since her arrival. "It's not as masculine as it used to be."

"I could see the wisdom in Mina's ideas," Benjamin said. "Women enjoy getting away to the mountains, too, and now they'll feel more comfortable here. When I first opened this place I catered to hunters and fishermen. They usually left their wives at home. These days the wives come along. I'm not a stick in the mud, you know. I can change with the times."

"Lauren," Amina said, "let me show you the new kitchen."

Benjamin laughed shortly. "We'll skip that, if you don't mind. Come with me, Colton."

While Lauren and Amina went off to explore the kitchen, Benjamin led Colton to the lounge. Unlike the lobby, the lounge was more laid-back and was the designated place for guests to have a cocktail or catch a game on TV. It looked like a large den except there was a fully stocked bar in the back and a burly bartender ready to mix your favorite libation.

"What's your poison?" Benjamin asked as he and Colton took seats at the bar.

"I'm not much of a drinker," Colton said. "How about the house beer?"

"Two drafts, George," said Benjamin.

George, a tall black guy in his late forties, must have weighed three hundred pounds, but it was distributed in such a way that he just looked stocky rather than overweight. "Anything you say, Ben," he said with a smile.

"George, this is Colton Riley," Benjamin introduced them. He glanced at Colton. "George has been with me for ten years. He's my right-hand man."

"Which is Ben's way of saying I do a little bit of everything around here," George joked as he drew two beers from a steel keg under the counter.

He set the mugs of beer before them. Foam spilled over the tops, and he wiped it away with a white dish towel.

"Thank you," said Colton.

"My pleasure," said George good-naturedly and turned away to fill another guest's order.

Colton and Benjamin drank their cold beers companionably before Ben broke the silence. "So, Colton, you and Laurie seem to be going strong."

"That's the first time I've ever heard anyone call Lauren Laurie," Colton commented.

"I'm the only one who calls her that," said Benjamin. "All the other girls have their names shortened, but no one ever called Lauren by a nickname. I don't know why. Maybe because she was the oldest. She was a serious child. Her grandmother used to say Laurie was so serious-minded. And that she did everything fast, from taking her first steps as a toddler to saying her first words. I don't know much about the hierarchy of siblings, but maybe my wife had a point. Laurie didn't spend much time doing childish things. That's why I'm glad to see her looking so relaxed and happy. You've no doubt had something to do with that, so I thank you."

Colton was looking into Ben's dark brown eyes and wondering what had brought this on. "If anyone's benefited from our relationship it's me. She makes me happy."

Ben smiled and changed the subject. "So, when was the last time you saw my big-headed son-in-law?"

Colton chuckled. "A couple of Sundays ago," he said. "He and Mrs. Gaines are doing well."

"Has he found a hobby since he retired?"

"He watches a lot of sports."

"He needs to get a job. My Virginia still works."

"Lauren says the general retired after more than thirty years of emeritus service, that's what's on the award he received when he retired."

"A man has the right to retire," Ben told him, explaining himself. "But Fonzi is not the type who can sit at home. He needs to be doing something productive. He hasn't been retired long enough to realize that. He will one day and if he hasn't already gone stir crazy, he'll find something to do."

"I get the feeling," Colton said, looking at Benjamin suspiciously, "that you don't dislike Mr. Gaines as much as you pretend to."

Benjamin laughed shortly. "I don't dislike him at all. He's been a good husband and father. That's all you can ask of a man. We've been sparring together for so long it's become a habit. He'd probably think I was sick or something if I didn't give him a hard time."

"And you're not mad at him for not giving you a grandson?"

"I would be one sorry son of a bitch not to be grateful for my wonderful granddaughters. They're all exceptional women. But I would be lying if I said I wasn't looking forward to having grandsons one day." He winked at Colton.

Colton laughed. "You're winking at the wrong man. Lauren and I are a long way from having kids."

"But you are heading in that direction, aren't you?" Ben asked hopefully.

"I am," Colton assured him. "I don't know if Lauren is."

"Are you going to do a little sightseeing on this visit?" Amina asked over dinner. "Or are you just going to spend all your time holed up in the cabin?" She wiggled her brows at Lauren in a leering manner.

Lauren laughed at her sister's antics then promptly ignored the innuendos. "I thought I'd take Colton to see Mingo Falls tomorrow."

"It ought to be pretty up there this time of year," Ben said. "Remember, though, the hike leading to the falls can be treacherous for those who're not used to the terrain. So be careful."

"Isn't that on the Cherokee Indian Reservation?" Colton asked.

"Yeah, *mingo* means *big bear* in Cherokee. Mingo Falls is one of the highest falls in the area," Ben answered before putting a large piece of steak he'd speared with his fork into his mouth.

"We don't need special permission to go on the reservation?"

"No, you don't need a permit," Ben said.

"Then let's do it," Colton said to Lauren.

Mingo Falls was located on the Qualla Boundary on the Cherokee Indian Reservation and just outside of the Great Smoky Mountains National Park which was the most visited National Park in the United States. Lauren and Colton were able to drive the SUV to Mingo Falls Campground but from there they had to walk.

The midmorning air was chilly, and fog could be seen in low-lying areas. The mist rose in the mountain air but it began to dissipate by late morning. The sky looked gray and the clouds portended rain.

Lauren and Colton wore sturdy walking shoes, jeans and T-shirts and jackets. In their backpacks they carried bottled water and a light lunch in the form of ham sandwiches and fresh peaches.

The climb to the falls was steep and the terrain was rocky and covered with tree roots that made it tricky to walk. It was necessary to be as careful as Ben had warned. As they strolled along the trail they encountered other hikers coming down, and when they looked back they saw others ascending. They heard the falls before they saw them. There was something spiritual about the sound of water falling over rocks.

When they finally reached the falls, they stood rapt with wonder at the one-hundred-and-twenty-foot example of nature's power and majesty.

Lauren stood in front of Colton, who had his arms wrapped around her. "No wonder people risk broken bones to get up here," Colton said softly. "This is breathtaking."

The crashing of the waterfall nearly drowned out his voice, but Lauren heard him and wholeheartedly agreed. "It seems like the most beautiful places on earth require effort to get to." She sighed wistfully. "Wouldn't it be great waking up in the morning and seeing that sight first thing?"

"If you designed the house," Colton told her, his cheek pressed to hers. "I'd gladly build it."

Lauren laughed. "It would take an architectural genius to design a house that would not only be able to be built on rocky terrain but have form and function."

"Then why don't we simply build a house together in Raleigh?" Colton suggested.

Lauren craned her neck to look back at him. "Are we building castles or are we being serious here?"

"We're doing both," he said. He carefully turned her around to face him, his hands on her upper arms so that they both kept their balance.

"I love you, Lauren," he said, looking deeply into her eyes.

Lauren was elated. She loved him, too, and she had hoped that he shared the same feelings but she'd been afraid to tell him how she felt. "I'm so relieved I'm not in this alone," she whispered. "I love you so much."

As they looked intensely into each other's eyes, Colton wanted to freeze the moment and keep it this way forever. She loved him. He could die happy.

But then loose rocks above began rolling toward them and suddenly their footing was not so sure after all. They fell and began sliding down the rocky incline they'd been standing on. Because he was heavier, Colton was rolling downward faster than Lauren. He tried to hold on to her as they fell, but the momentum made it impossible to do so. Lauren felt their fingers disconnect. She was trying not to panic. Luckily, they weren't near a cliff. Eventually, their descent would stop and they would be able to get back up and walk out of here.

She was right. Colton ended up bumping into a huge outgrowth of a pine tree's roots and as she was rolling past him he reached out and grabbed her, thereby stopping her descent.

For a few minutes all they could do was hold each other and catch their breaths. She looked him over. He had scratches on his face but he looked none the worse for wear. As he looked back at her, the expression in his gray eyes went from concerned to relieved.

"You've got a scratch across your left eyebrow," he said, "otherwise you look okay. How do you feel?"

She managed a weak smile. "I don't think anything's broken. How about you?"

Colton's one dimple winked at her. "Never better," he said. "Do you see what falling for you gets me?"

They rose carefully to their feet. "You're so corny," Lauren said of his "falling for you" comment.

"If we make it back to the cabin I'm going to show you corny," he promised.

"You mean *when* we make it back to the cabin," she corrected him.

"Yes, ma'am," Colton said with a smile.

Hand in hand, they slowly made their way back up to the path where they encountered a couple about to embark on the same trail. The couple eyed them with curiosity. Lauren imagined they had dirt and leaves stuck on their clothes to say nothing of the scratches marring exposed skin.

"Are you okay?" the woman asked.

"The rocks are a bit loose back there," Colton told them. "So watch your step."

They continued walking. They heard the woman say to her partner, "Maybe we ought to turn back."

But her partner pooh-poohed her misgivings.

Lauren squeezed Colton's hand. "Hear that? I brought you here and almost got you killed but it was worth it."

Colton glanced down at her, his eyes alight with humor. "You told me you loved me. That was worth it."

Lauren grinned. "You say the sweetest things."

An hour or so later they were soaking in the sunken tub of Lauren's cabin playing footsies. "I'm worried about what could happen to you…now that I love you and you know it," Lauren said as her right foot found a sensitive area of his body and gently caressed it with her toes.

Colton was finding it difficult to think with her foot where it was. "What do you mean?"

"I told you about the curse, didn't I?"

He'd had his eyes closed enjoying the moment. But now he opened them and looked at her. "I thought you didn't believe in it."

"I don't," she said, "But I also didn't believe I'd ever meet a decent man and fall in love. And here we are."

"You have a way of making your life harder than it needs to be," Colton said as he sat up on his end of the tub and removed her foot from his crotch. "I command you to think only positive thoughts for the rest of the weekend." He pulled her toward him and she climbed on top of him, water splashing over the sides of the tub to the floor. He squeezed her bottom with both hands as their groins rubbed together in the warm soapy water. Lauren cooed with delight. This was infinitely better than tumbling down a hill in a national forest, she thought.

Colton had been semierect throughout their playful foreplay. Now he was fully erect and ready for her to impale herself on him. But Lauren had other ideas. She reached behind him and pulled the tub's plug. Then she kissed him briefly and got up. Thanks to the nonslip ridges in the tub's bottom she didn't fear falling when she grabbed his hand and coaxed him to his feet. "Let's move this to the bedroom, okay? I'm cold."

He was happy to oblige her. In fact, he took great pleasure in taking the removable showerhead and rinsing the suds off her beautiful brown body, then patting her down with a fluffy white towel. He liked pampering her. If she'd let him, he'd wash her hair, but Lauren had a thing about her hair. She was tender-headed and didn't trust he'd be gentle—something about his big man hands. He smiled as he held her bathrobe for her and she slipped inside it. She rose up on her tip-toes and kissed his chin. "Your turn," she murmured, her voice sexy. She dried him off and held his robe open for him in return. After he was ensconced in its warmth he bent and swept her into his arms and carried her to the adjoining bedroom.

Lauren giggled. "Don't drop me. I've been beat up enough for one day."

"I'm not going to drop you, woman, but I do believe you've put on a few pounds lately."

"I weigh the same as I did the day we met," Lauren claimed. "But if I have gained a few you can blame yourself, Mr. Gourmet Chef."

Colton dropped her onto the bed and turned to remove his robe and deposit it on the floor. Turning back he watched her as she followed his every movement. He liked it when she couldn't draw her eyes away from him.

Lauren removed her robe and tossed it onto a nearby chair. She moved backward on the bed, her eyes riveted on Colton's cinnamon-brown body, the muscles rippling enticingly as he walked toward her. "Like what you see?" he asked as he straddled her and forced her legs apart.

Lauren arched her back, her pelvis thrust upward. "You're so damned vain. Maybe I simply admire the human body in all its aesthetic beauty, much like, as an architect, I admire a beautiful building."

Colton chuckled. "Or maybe looking at me makes you wet and horny as hell."

"Must you be so crude?" she asked, pretending to be aghast at his choice of words.

"Too titillating for you?" he asked as he bent and licked the nipple of her right breast. His hot tongue laved the hardened nipple until Lauren writhed with pent-up sexual desire. He paid equal attention to the left nipple. Then he kissed his way down past her rib cage to her belly and farther still until he was feasting on her feminine center with abandon.

Lauren moaned loudly. Her inhibitions were long gone and her will abolished under the assault of his mouth. She came with a shout and even then Colton didn't let up, but only slowed down to coincide with her trembling release.

"I love you, I love you, I love you," she cried repeatedly.

That only increased his ardor. His penis was hard and throbbing, and by the time he got a condom on he could barely contain the need to enter her. She was more than ready for him and he slipped inside, her folds welcoming him with hot intensity. Lauren clung to him, her legs wrapped tightly around him. His thrusts were so deep she felt he might tear her asunder but at that moment all she cared about was the pleasure of loving him and being loved by him. She grabbed his ass with both hands and held on. She could feel his muscles flexing as he moved. The hot steel of his shaft filled her up.

The walls of her vagina quivered with the lovely friction. She felt another orgasm coming on and at the same time that Colton growled his release, she exploded again. Together, they fell onto the bed and faced one another, smiling gently, breathing hard.

"I like this much better than hiking," she told him sincerely.

Colton laughed. "I'll keep that in mind."

Chapter 14

Their weekend in the mountains would be the last vacation they would be able to take for months to come. Work kept them extremely busy. The building business was booming due to the improved economy and both Lauren and Colton benefited from it. In October, Lawrence, Mayer and McGill, pleased with Lauren's work on the children's hospital, offered her a partnership, which she accepted. She also hired an intern, a twenty-year-old African American woman named Deanna Lane, who was currently attending Duke University.

Colton, who usually thrived on getting out in the field, found himself more and more in the office with clients. He missed the physical labor but knew as head of the company he had to show leadership and keep them fiscally strong. That meant he had to court clients and once he landed them, keep them happy and eager to do business with them over and over again. Now he knew what his father meant when he'd said that you always had to have your business cap on.

As for his love life, it remained hot and heavy. They'd exchanged keys and it wasn't unusual for Lauren to come home from work and find him in her kitchen preparing a meal for them.

On the night before Thanksgiving, Colton came home and found Lauren not in his tub but asleep in his bed. He stood there smiling at the image she made, like a black Goldilocks snoozing away while the big bad bear arrived home and discovered her in his bed. He got undressed and climbed in with her. She awakened as soon as he knelt on the bed, and blinked at him. Smiling, she murmured, "You're home."

He kissed her and pulled her close, pulling the covers over both of them. "It's cold outside."

She snuggled into him, her warm, naked body molding itself to him. "But it's warm in here."

"Not that I'm not happy to see you," he said, looking into her eyes, "but you said you and your sisters were spending the night at your parents' house to help your mother prepare Thanksgiving dinner."

"I know I did," she said softly, "and I meant to, but Momma nixed that. She said it's time we started cooking dinner ourselves and inviting her and Daddy to our houses. So Desiree volunteered for duty. We're all going to her house tomorrow for dinner."

"Isn't that a lot of cooking on Desiree?"

"Desi's not cooking. Don't tell Momma but she got on the phone with a caterer the minute after she told us she'd handle it. She's organized like that."

"Yay, Desiree," Colton said. "Now, come here."

Benjamin closed the lodge for Thanksgiving, so he and Amina drove to Raleigh to spend time with the family. His old blue Ford pickup was parked in Desiree's driveway when Lauren and Colton arrived the next day at noon. It looked out of place next to the other late-model cars and SUVs.

Desiree met them at the door looking cool and collected and chic in a royal-blue dress and black patent leather pumps. Lauren kissed her proffered cheek. "You didn't say anything about dressing up."

She and Colton wore casual clothes. He was in navy blue Dockers and a white short-sleeved shirt, a black hoodie and athletic shoes. She wore black slacks and a lavender pullover top, a black hoodie and athletic shoes.

Desiree looked her over. "You look great. I'm a nervous wreck and I need my armor to get me through today. I've already been busted. Momma inspected the kitchen and found the containers the catered food came in. I'll never live it down."

Lauren laughed. "You're a psychotherapist. Don't you have some kind of psychological trick that'll get you through today?"

"Yes," Desiree said, "and it involves mimosas. I've got a pitcher mixed in the kitchen. Help yourself."

Lauren looked closely at her sister's eyes. They were a little glazed. "Desi, are you drunk?"

Desiree smiled. "That's a possibility."

Desiree closed the front door after Lauren and Colton were inside then gestured to the great room to the left of the foyer, which served as the entertainment room. "Everybody's in there. Make yourselves comfortable while I go check on the rolls I put in the oven a few minutes ago."

Desiree's home was immaculate like its owner. The air was redolent with enticing aromas of food cooking. Two-stories, it had high ceilings, hardwood floors throughout except for tile in the kitchen and baths. She liked open spaces so the rooms were tastefully decorated with minimalist furnishings in modern styles. Knickknacks were few and far between but she had a penchant for African American artists like Romare Bearden. Prints of his watercolors could be found above the fireplace in the spacious living room and on her bedroom wall.

Lauren and Colton were greeted as soon as they entered the great room. Virginia and Fonzi were sitting on the couch with Amina between them. Benjamin sat in a chair across from them and Meghan sat on the arm of her grandfather's chair. There was a football game on TV.

Amina got up to hug Lauren. "I haven't seen you since April," Lauren cried. She took in Amina's huge Afro. "You look like that jazz artist, what's her name?"

"Esperanza Spalding," Meghan spoke up from her perch on the arm of Benjamin's chair. "I love her."

Lauren touched her sister's hair. "You look fierce!"

"Thanks," Amina said. "I'm having fun being natural these days. My hair feels so much stronger in its natural state."

"How is life in the mountains? Have you met any nice guys?"

Amina laughed. "If I were looking for a guy I'd be out of luck up there. They're either married or Grandpa's age."

Benjamin heard that and had to add, "She's not lying. I told her a guy's going to have to drop out of the sky for her."

"Mina's not looking for a man. She's there to learn the business. How is that part going?" Virginia interjected.

"She's smart as all get-out," Benjamin said proudly. "She already knows more than I know about customer relations. The guests love her. She's going to be just fine, Virginia."

Virginia sat back on the couch beside Fonzi, satisfied with her father's assessment of his granddaughter.

"Enough about me," said Amina, her teasing gaze encompassing Lauren and Colton. "How are you two doing? You haven't taken anymore spills since Mingo Falls, have you?"

"No, thank goodness," Lauren answered for both of them. "We've stayed out of the woods."

"This is the first I've heard of an incident involving you and Colton at Mingo Falls," Virginia said, her eyes on Lauren. "When were you there?"

"In April," Lauren answered easily. "We went to Bryson City for the weekend."

"You'd only known one another four months at that time," Virginia commented.

Lauren's face went hot with embarrassment. Surely her mother wasn't going to discuss her sex life in front of everyone.

"Ginny," Fonzi said in warning tones.

But Virginia would not be muzzled. "Am I the only one in this family who thinks their relationship is going too fast?"

She turned to Fonzi. "You don't think that Lauren needs to get her head together before getting too emotionally attached to Colton? She just got out of a marriage."

"Mother, I'm standing right here. If you have a problem with me, please direct your comments to me."

"I don't like your tone of voice, young lady," Virginia told her, standing up to face her. Lauren was nearly a foot taller than her mother.

"And I don't like yours," Lauren said respectfully. "How can you possibly have a problem with my relationship with Colton? He's been nothing but a gentleman."

Virginia turned to look at Colton who had taken a seat on the chair beside Benjamin's. "You're a good man. I know that. I have no problem with you. I have a problem with my daughter getting out of one marriage and immediately getting involved with another man. A decent man whose heart she might break when she discovers that she's not ready to be everything he needs her to be. Mainly because she hasn't yet resolved issues relating to her recent marriage." Her gaze back on Lauren now, she continued, "You haven't been divorced a year. Are you over Adam?"

Lauren's eyes bugged out. Her mother obviously didn't care that she was embarrassing her in front of Colton.

"I could tell you things about Adam that would curl your hair and you would never again doubt that I'm completely over him," Lauren said, her voice strangled. "But I won't do that here and now. That's private and actually, it's none of your business. I love you, Momma, but you're too hard on the people you care about. Is it any wonder none of your daughters have been able to find happiness with a man?"

She hadn't meant to say that, but there it was. She couldn't take it back. Her expression remorseful, she said, "That didn't come out right. I didn't mean to suggest it's your fault, but we are always aiming for perfection because of your influence and because we don't want to disappoint you. My God, I stayed with Adam longer than I should have because I didn't want to admit defeat. You and Daddy told me before I married him that he couldn't be trusted and I married him anyway. Do you know how badly I felt when the marriage failed? It meant I would have to hear 'I told you so' from you, Momma!"

Desiree had entered the room in the middle of Lauren's speech and Meghan, who hated to see anyone upset in the family, was wildly gesturing to her to step in with professional advice. When Desiree remained silent, Meghan cried, "Desi, do something. Tell Lauren she's wrong about Momma."

Desiree went to put her arm about Lauren's shoulders. She looked at Amina, who had gotten to her feet, as well. "Mina, is Lauren wrong?"

Amina went to stand on the other side of Lauren in a show of support. "No, she's not wrong." She directed her next comment to her youngest sister, Meghan. "Maybe by the time you came along Momma had run out of steam. But she was hard on us, always pitting us against each other to compete for her affections. To prove that we were good girls, smart girls, put on this earth to achieve the highest possible goals in life. Me? I was going to be a general like my father." She looked her mother in the eyes. "Sorry to disappoint you, Momma."

Desiree and Lauren hugged her tightly. Meghan got up and joined her sisters. She had tears in her eyes. "I'm sorry," she whispered over and over again.

"What is this, Beat Up On Your Mother Day?" asked Virginia incredulously. Her petite body practically trembled with indignation. "If I was hard on you girls it was because I wanted you to believe in yourselves, to know that you could accomplish anything. That's what a parent's supposed to do, inspire and cheer her children on. Apparently it worked. I got an architect, a psychotherapist, a zoologist, an accountant and a college professor out of it."

Benjamin suddenly stood up and grabbed Virginia by the shoulders and shook her. "Are you not hearing what they're saying, Virginia? You've alienated your children by being a hard-ass. Is that plain enough English for you?"

Virginia looked crestfallen. "Daddy, please don't say that. I love my children!"

"I know you love them, but you're driving them away with your attitude." He sighed heavily. "Baby girl, if I did anything to you when you were growing up to make you behave this way, I'm sorry." He let go of her and went on to explain as everyone gathered around him and Virginia, "I wasn't always as successful as I am now. When Virginia was a child her mother and I struggled. She even went hungry sometimes. I don't know, maybe the memory of hard times made her believe she had to push her daughters to succeed so they'd never have to go through what she did. I don't know for sure." He turned to Virginia once more and smiled. "But deep down she's got a good heart. She really does believe she does what she does for the betterment of her family."

Fonzi, who was nearby, spoke up on his wife's behalf. "If you girls want to blame anyone, blame me. I was often away from home and Ginny had to do everything by herself. I'm the one who turned her into an iron soldier."

Virginia was crying silently. Fonzi hugged her close. "It's always best to get things out in the open, sweetheart. The girls aren't saying they don't love you."

Lauren, Amina, Meghan and Desiree wrapped their arms around their parents in a group hug.

Colton, standing beside Benjamin, joked, "Are all Thanksgivings with the Gaineses like this?"

Ben looked up at him and laughed, "No, this is a first. But I have a good feeling about it."

Later that night in bed at Colton's house, he held Lauren close after making love. Colton peered lovingly into her eyes. Her hair was a tangled mess. He liked it that way. Today had been enlightening. It wasn't because of the argument he'd witnessed between Lauren and her mother. He knew that no family was perfect. Every family was dysfunctional in one way or another.

What he had found interesting was the ease with which they had forgiven each other and gone on to have a wonderful time together. Some families let grudges grow and they feuded for years.

Lauren smiled at him. "What're you thinking?"

"That your family and my family are a lot alike," he said softly.

"Oh, your family's nuts, too?" she joked.

"You have an idealized view of my mom and dad because you saw them in a relaxed environment in the mountains. I saw them every day growing up. They argued as much as any other couple. But after they argued, they made up and there was never any fear of them breaking up. They were in it together, forever. That's what I want for you and me."

"I want that, too," she told him, "more than anything."

"Then let's do it," Colton said, his eyes sweeping

over her face. "I think it would be romantic to get married a year from the day we met."

Lauren gasped. "Are you asking me to marry you?"

Colton laughed shortly. "Don't look so shocked. Yes, I am. I'm sorry for the circumstances, being naked in bed and all that. But this wasn't planned, it just came out. I've never asked anyone to marry me before." He reached over and opened the top drawer in the nightstand on his side of the bed and withdrew a small brown velvet jewelry box. "I do have the ring, though. I bought it weeks ago and have been trying to think of a romantic way to propose but I kept drawing a blank."

While he was rambling on, Lauren sat up in bed, snatched the jewelry box from his clutches and tore it open. She stared down at a five-carat solitaire in a platinum setting. Looking at him with an astonished expression, she cried, "You're serious!"

"As serious as a naked man can be," he said, sitting up, as well. He took the jewelry box back, plucked the ring from it and placed it on her finger. It was a perfect fit. "You are a six. That was the jeweler's guess after I described you."

Lauren continued to regard him with a shocked expression. He cleared his throat. "I never thought you'd be at a loss for words. Say something, anything. Okay, not anything. I'm hoping for a positive response."

Tears pooled in her eyes and left wet trails down her cheeks. "Yes, I'll marry you."

She threw her arms around his neck. "You know

we can never tell anyone how you proposed. We're going to have to make something up."

Colton grinned and kissed her. "It'll be our secret."

Lauren stood in the atrium of the new children's hospital. Sunlight spilled in from the glass dome above. She couldn't believe the project was so close to completion. It had been nearly a year since they'd broken ground.

It was a Sunday and the construction crew was not there. She walked the building alone, marveling at the realization of what had once only been in her mind.

"Hey, Lauren, I see great minds think alike."

She turned around to find Adam walking toward her. She immediately grew tense.

He must have seen it in her face because he quickly said, "Don't worry. I'm not here to make a scene. I saw your car and debated whether I should come in or not. I saw your wedding announcement in the paper and I wanted to wish you well."

Lauren didn't know what to make of him. She decided to take the high road and be civil. "Thank you, Adam."

He took a deep breath and visibly relaxed. Looking up at the glass dome above their heads, he said, "Great project, huh? It turned out better than I imagined."

Lauren smiled. "I have to agree. Your company did a good job."

He smiled his thanks. Then he turned to leave. "I've got to go. Nichole is cooking dinner."

Lauren couldn't let that comment go unnoticed. "Nichole?"

He smiled. "Yes, I apologized and asked her to take me back and she forgave me. We're engaged."

Lauren was genuinely surprised. "Good for you," she said, and meant it.

He smiled and gave her a salute as he continued on his way.

Lauren finished her tour of the building alone.

Chapter 15

The club was on the seedy side of town and was not the type of establishment Colton would typically be willing to go to. But then he hadn't chosen it. His best man, Decker, had. Decker and several of the other men who'd been invited to his bachelor party were onstage gyrating with scantily clad strippers. Decker had rented the place out, as well as the services of the strippers, for the night.

The music was so loud Colton couldn't hear himself think.

A bra landed on his head, and he brushed it off onto the floor. Decker came down off the stage and plopped down across from him. "Look, cuz, this party is supposed to be for you and you're sitting there nursing a beer. Get up and dance."

"I'm danced out," Colton told him. He glanced at his watch. "It's three in the morning. Don't you think it's time to wrap up the party and head home? My wedding is in eleven hours."

Decker, who was about three sheets to the wind, sighed loudly. "You're not even married yet and she's got you on a leash."

"Nobody's got me on a leash," Colton denied. "I simply know who I am and it's not this. When you asked me what I wanted to do for my bachelor party I told you I wanted to go to a sports bar and watch a couple games with the guys. Why you kids think naked women doing degrading things is the ultimate bachelor party, I'll never know."

"Because for those of us who aren't already hog-tied, naked women doing degrading things *is* the ultimate in a bachelor party," Decker said.

"That's just why Desiree won't go out with you."

"Don't mention that devil's spawn. I ran into her at a Starbucks the other day and she was so friendly, smiling and asking me how life had been treating me but when I asked her to sit down and have a coffee with me she said she had an appointment."

"Don't call her devil's spawn just because she won't go out with you. She has her reasons."

"Such as?" asked Decker sarcastically.

"It's not for me to say," Colton told him. "You'll have to ask her yourself."

"I don't care what her reasons are," Decker declared and went back onstage where a buxom blonde threw a feather boa around his neck and pulled him against her chest. He turned his head, grinned at Colton and gave him a thumbs-up. "A girl's got to make a living!" he yelled.

Colton laughed.

"Having fun?" asked a sultry feminine voice at Colton's side.

He looked up at the curvaceous brunette and smiled. "Just great, thanks." He returned his attention to the stage, hoping she'd get the hint and leave him alone.

Instead, she sat down in the chair Decker had vacated earlier. "My name's Viveca," she told him. "If this scene isn't your cup of tea, we can go somewhere private."

"Thanks, but I'm engaged," Colton said firmly.

"I know," she said. "You're the guest of honor." Her gaze went to Decker.

"Oh, he told you to take care of me, huh?" Colton guessed.

She smiled seductively. "He was very generous."

That did it. Colton got up and walked onto the stage and dragged Decker off of it. He pulled him back to the table where the brunette was still sitting.

"Did you tell her to entertain me?" he asked Decker through clenched teeth.

Decker shook his hands off him. "Can't you take a joke, cuz? I knew you'd never cheat on Lauren. But it's traditional for the groom to be offered the opportunity to have another woman before he gets tied down to one woman for the rest of his life."

"Desiree was right," Colton told him. "You're not ready for her. I'm out of here."

"But you're my ride home," Decker protested.

Colton headed for the exit. "If I'm giving you a lift you'd better come on."

Decker started yelling to the other guys who'd been invited to the bachelor party, "Hey, fellas, we're taking off."

"Yeah," Colton yelled, too, wondering why he was even bothering to thank them for coming when all of them were so drunk they wouldn't remember his words tomorrow. "Thanks for coming!"

As he walked out the door of the establishment, he didn't bother to look back to see if his cousin was following him. In the parking lot, which was poorly lit, he went to his car and unlocked the door.

He heard a noise behind him and thinking it was Decker he whirled around to tell him to get in the car. But it wasn't Decker. It was a stranger and he was wielding a crowbar like a weapon. Colton was able to block the blow and grab the crowbar. He wrenched it out of the guy's grasp and swung it, hitting the guy on the forearm as he held up his arm to protect his head.

"Ah!" the guy yelled. "Don't hurt me. I'm sorry, I'm sorry. Please don't hurt me."

Colton finally got a good look at the man. He was thin and bedraggled. His hair was matted and he looked and smelled like he hadn't bathed in a long time.

"Cuz, what the hell's going on?" Decker cried as he ran toward Colton.

"I was attacked," Colton said, pointing the crowbar at the man who'd jumped him. "Call the police."

"Please mister, I was hungry," the man said.

Decker was already punching in the numbers on his cell phone.

Suddenly, a car came careening straight at them. The assailant ran, screaming his head off. Colton wound up tackling Decker, who had frozen in the headlights, and shoving him out of the way just in time. They ended up sprawled on their sides in the alley next to a Dumpster.

Decker got to his feet but Colton didn't get up. Decker knelt over his cousin. "Colton?" Colton didn't answer. Decker gently rolled him onto his back. Colton was unconscious and there was a gash on the side of his head. It appeared he'd hit his head on the Dumpster when he'd propelled both of them out of the path of the car that had tried to run them down.

Decker had dropped his cell phone when Colton had shoved him out of harm's way. He doubled back and found it lying on the pavement in pieces. He had no alternative but to run back into the club and make a call from there.

He looked back at Colton lying in that dirty alleyway one more time before sprinting toward the club's entrance.

Decker had phoned Lauren from the hospital as he sat in the emergency room waiting area. Half an hour later she arrived and was told the same thing Decker had been told earlier. Colton was still unconscious and they were doing everything in their power to bring him around.

Lauren paced the floor, unable to sit for any length of time. Decker sat feeling guilty for having taken his cousin to a strip club in a bad neighborhood.

A few minutes after Lauren had gotten to the hospital Desiree and Meghan showed up. Embarrassed about his part in the drama and knowing he must smell like a distillery, Decker was not overly enthusiastic about seeing them, especially Desiree. He had to repeat the story of how they'd come to be at the hospital. He imagined Desiree would dislike him even more than she already did after tonight.

About two hours after Colton had been brought in, a doctor in scrubs strode into the emergency room waiting area and asked for the family of Colton Riley. They all approached her with hopeful looks on their faces.

"He's awake," she reported. "There doesn't seem to be any permanent damage but head wounds can be tricky. We're keeping him overnight for observation."

"Thank you, Doctor," Lauren said gratefully. "Can we see him?"

The doctor smiled. "Only one of you, I'm afraid."

Lauren followed the doctor back to an examining room. She found Colton lying on his back in a narrow hospital bed. He smiled when he spotted her. "Hey, baby."

The doctor left them alone and Lauren hurried to his side.

She grasped his hand in hers and kissed his cheek. "You gave me quite the scare."

He smiled weakly. "You thought it was the curse all over again for a minute there, huh?"

"Don't even joke about that."

His gray eyes were alight with humor. "I would have to be dead to miss our wedding tomorrow."

"Stop talking," Lauren ordered him with tears in her eyes. "Do you realize what our lives were like a year ago? Frank had recently died and I was a basket case over a failed marriage. Never joke about dying. I don't know what I'd do if I lost you."

He squeezed her hand. "I'm not going anywhere."

Meanwhile in the waiting room, Desiree had sat down beside Decker. Meghan had gone in search of coffee.

"It's a good thing you were with Colton when he got hurt," she said, drawing him into a conversation. She had good instincts and knew he was blaming himself for Colton's injuries.

She wondered if she wanted to ease his pain because that was her profession, or if she was actually starting to like him.

At any rate he seemed vulnerable and she'd never been able to resist helping anyone in a weakened state.

He looked at her. "You don't have to be nice to me. I know you can't stand me."

"That isn't true, Decker," she denied. The truth was she didn't think of him at all. She couldn't say that though. It would be cruel. She didn't waste time thinking about the handsome attorney because she'd pegged him as a player from their first meeting and she had no patience with men who didn't respect women. It wasn't personal.

"I'm going to tell you something, and I hope you'll try to understand. I've been avoiding you because I have a low tolerance for men who see women as playthings. I have nothing against you. You seem like a decent guy except for the player vibe you give off. But, you see, I've had a great guy in my life and I know what I want in a man. He died a few years ago and, I'm sorry, but I've been comparing every guy I meet to him and they never stack up."

Decker just smiled at her. He knew now that he'd never win her heart. What live man could compete with the memory of a lost love?

Colton's doctor signed his release papers at ten the next morning. He was told to take it easy for a couple of days but there should be no permanent damage from his head injury.

Lauren told him they could postpone the wedding until he was fully recovered but he insisted he was fine. He could rest after the wedding.

She'd stared into his eyes as if she could discern his sincerity. He'd grinned at her. "You're just going to have to take my word for it."

She relented but promised to watch him like a hawk.

They reluctantly separated after she saw him home from the hospital. She would be at her parents' house where her mother and her sisters, including Petra, who was flying in from West Africa, would help her get ready for the wedding. The next time they would see each other would be at St. Paul AME Church, the same church where they'd had Frank's memorial service. Colton's mother had been pleased with their decision to be married there. She said it would almost feel as if Frank would be there.

Back at the Gaineses' house, Lauren sat at her mother's vanity table while Virginia put the finishing touches on her upswept hairstyle. Since their blowout on Thanksgiving Day the two of them had been less reticent with one another. Clearing the air had been a cathartic experience.

Virginia smiled at her daughter's reflection in the mirror. For her afternoon wedding Lauren had chosen not a gown but a cocktail-length dress in cream. It was sleeveless and the hem fell just above her knees. V-necked, it revealed only a glimpse of cleavage, and the waist was fitted. The soft folds of the skirt swirled about her hips and thighs. It was like wearing a confection.

"You make a beautiful bride, sweetheart," Virginia said, a lump forming in her throat. "I'm so pleased for you. I know you and Colton will be happy together."

Lauren rose and hugged her mother. "Thanks, Momma. That means a lot to me." Tears fell. Virginia took her handkerchief that she kept in her cleavage and patted them away. "None of that now," she admonished. "Today is for smiling and laughing, not crying."

"Yeah," Petra cried, coming to hug her mother and sister. "The second time is the charm!"

Lauren laughed at her petite sister. Of the five of them she was the shortest at only five-three. But Petra was still three inches taller than their mother. She had their mother's natural hair color, too, a deep brown that almost looked black.

It was wavy and long like Lauren's but unlike Lauren she'd never cut hers and it fell to her waist.

Desiree entered the room issuing orders. "Five minutes before we get into the cars and head to the church, so make sure you have everything ready to go."

"I'd better go check on your father," Virginia announced. "That man can't tie his tie without me."

All five sisters were dressed in cocktail-length dresses. Lauren had not chosen the styles and colors for her sisters, just the length. She'd left the styles and colors up to them because they knew best what they looked good in and she wanted them to feel beautiful on her special day, too.

They huddled together in their parents' bedroom. "Shall we pray that the honeymoon will be productive and make us aunts?" Petra asked jokingly.

"Yes," Meghan said, "because our older sister isn't getting any younger and Momma and Daddy want grandkids soon. Plus Grandpa Beck's been waiting for a male child to be born into this family for years and he's nearly eighty."

"Will you selfish creatures leave my uterus alone?" Lauren chimed in. "If you must pray for something, pray for good weather today. God will send me a child when He sees fit."

The weather was gorgeous. The December air was crisp and cool. The sun shone brightly and there was a light breeze that ruffled the skirts of the ladies' dresses and caused the gentlemen who wore hats to hang on to them.

Three hundred guests filled the pews of St. Paul AME church. Organ music resounded off the walls of the magnificent edifice.

The general wore his dress uniform as he escorted Lauren down the aisle. He looked very handsome.

Lauren's maid of honor was Desiree. Colton's best man, Decker, could not keep his eyes off her.

Colton, looking resplendent in his tuxedo, felt light-headed with love when he saw his bride walking down the aisle on her father's arm. She looked innocent, sexy and sophisticated all at once. When she saw him looking at her, she smiled and mouthed, "I love you." That made him inordinately happy.

After the minister pronounced them husband and wife, the kiss lasted nearly a full minute. Then Colton bent and picked up his bride and carried her back down the aisle to an enthusiastic applause. Laughing, Lauren gazed into her new husband's eyes and said, "Don't hurt yourself. You just got out of the hospital, remember?"

Colton grinned, "Be quiet, Mrs. Riley, and enjoy the ride. It's our wedding day!"

He carried her all the way down the church's front steps and to the waiting limousine, with friends and family cheering him on.

Just as he was about to deposit her onto the back seat of the limo, Lauren cried, "Wait, wait, the bouquet!"

Colton set her down on the sidewalk and she turned

her back to the crowd and tossed the bouquet over her head.

Her sisters were standing directly behind her but they all stepped aside, purposefully ducking out of the way of the flying bouquet, and Veronica wound up catching it. She laughed and held it up triumphantly, crowing, "There's some life left in the old girl yet!" which elicited laughter as they stood on the sidewalk waving goodbye to Lauren and Colton.

In the car, Colton pulled Lauren into his arms and kissed her soundly. When they parted he murmured against her cheek, "Dad must be laughing in heaven right about now."

"Why?" Lauren asked softly, her eyes sparkling with happiness.

"Because he and Mom were right. You and I were meant for each other."

* * * * *

REQUEST YOUR FREE BOOKS!

2 FREE NOVELS
PLUS 2 FREE GIFTS!

KIMANI™
ROMANCE

Love's ultimate destination!

KROM13R

Will she get past her
once-broken heart
and trust again?

KIMANI ROMANCE

Let me
Hold
You

Melanie Schuster

If Alana Sharp Dumond misses the feel of a man's arms around her,
she'll never admit it. Worldly restaurateur Roland Casey has had his
eye on Alana for months, but Alana keeps putting the brakes on all
his moves. Roland has no doubt that he can send her temperature
racing, but can he mend her once-broken heart?

Available October 2013
wherever books are sold!

KPMS3271013